THE BLOODLINE

The Friessens (Andy & Laura)

LORHAINNE ECKHART

The Bloodline Copyright © 2015 Lorhainne Ekelund
The Bloodline Paperback Copyright © 2016 Lorhainne Ekelund
Editor: Talia Leduc

All rights reserved.
ISBN-13: 978-1794052284

Give feedback on the book at:
lorhainneeckhart@hotmail.com

Twitter: @LEckhart
Facebook: AuthorLorhainneEckhart

Printed in the U.S.A

What reviewers are saying

"Who wouldn't want a man like Andy!"

Kindle Customer

*"Andy's story took me by surprise. This book says so much
more than just the words. It will make you think about
what's really important in life."*

Lora

Andy Friessen has two guarantees in life:

1. His wife, Laura, and his children are safe
   from the control of his family.

2. A safety deposit box holds evidence that
   could blow his mother's world apart.

But nothing is ever simple or easy, and one night tragedy strikes, yanking the rug from under him. This time, secrets and lies could destroy the solid foundation he's built for his family.

Chapter One

The numbers just weren't adding up. As Andy stared at the spreadsheet on his iMac, his eyes started to go blurry. He could just pass this off to his accountant, but he felt it was important to know every detail of his business before he contracted any work out. Right now, he was missing five more longhorns from the extensive herd he had amassed.

"Andy, do you want some tea?"

He didn't need to glance up to his wife, Laura, to know she was already bringing him some, the herbal kind he couldn't believe he actually liked. He leaned back in the dark leather chair behind his desk, neat and dust free, just the way he liked it.

"How did you know?" He took the steaming mug, breathing in the orange spice and taking a welcome sip.

Laura leaned down on the desk, resting her arms and just looking at him. She had such a soft smile, so genuine that she made him feel he could do anything. "Oh, you've been working in here for hours, holed up. Heard you swear a few times, so I knew things weren't quite working out the way you wanted." She had their baby monitor hooked to the waistband of her jeans—jeans she filled out in a way that drew every man's eye. Some women had great asses, and his wife was one of them.

She was a welcome distraction, considering there had seemed to be a constant loss of cattle over the past twelve weeks. "It'll be fine," he said. "The baby asleep?" He took another welcome sip as the warmth eased some of his frustration. So did she, the way she leaned on his desk, giving him an eyeful of her cleavage. Andy needed the distraction. He was getting worked up because someone or something was taking his cattle from him—taking what was his, what belonged to his family. Right now, someone was messing with his livelihood, and his next move would be to hire more help to find out what was happening to his sizeable herd: three hundred head of longhorns, including breeding stock and yearlings. It was the yearlings who were getting picked off.

"She went down about an hour ago," Laura said. "Sarah's so good, just like Chelsea. She's an angel, the way she sleeps on her side, her tiny little thumb in her mouth."

He didn't think he'd ever get tired of hearing everything about his children. Sarah, the baby, had been born eight weeks ago. It had been an easy birth. They'd made it to the hospital just in time, and Laura had eased through her contractions. Two hours later, Sarah had been born—an easy baby, a content baby, and the youngest of their four.

"What about the munchkins? No one's been bugging me," Andy said, not that he'd ever once considered his twins, Chelsea and Jeremy, who were just a few months shy of three, an annoyance. They were happy, healthy, full of life, radiating joy from their innocent smiles, which filled his heart so full at times he thought it would burst.

"Napping, too. Jeremy insisted he wasn't tired and argued with me up until he fell asleep, and that was before I even got Chelsea tucked in."

He reached out and skimmed his thumb over Laura's cheekbone, under her eyes. The dark circles she'd had from nursing the baby the first few weeks had disappeared, and she now had a healthy glow. Her blond hair had a natural wave it hadn't before, and it was pinned up in a messy bun that made her look gorgeous. Did she have any idea what she did to him? He doubted it. "So there's just you and me and a quiet house for..." He reached out, sliding his hand down Laura's side as she leaned on the desk beside him.

"What are you doing?" she teased as he put his tea down, and she straddled his lap, her arms linked around his neck.

He couldn't get over how well she fit him, how she moved against him, a touch, a breath. Giving herself to him was a gift he had once taken for granted. What a fool he'd been. Never again would he disrespect Laura or be ungrateful for all she had given him: his children, her love, herself. "Touching my wife," he said. Maybe it was arrogant and selfish, but he could only hold himself back from loving Laura for so long. He'd been patient for months during her late pregnancy and after, and he was making up for lost time, needing to bury himself in her heat, in her love, and connect with her.

He ran his large hand down her stomach, which still had a slight bulge from where she'd carried his children. It was a miracle how his seed had created the lives that filled this house, making it a home. His family.

Her breath hissed, and he could feel the way she trembled as he ran his hand up and over both her generous breasts, which fed his baby girl. His other hand followed as he shoved his fingers in her hair, pulling it loose, pulling her down so he could taste those full, kissable red lips.

Her eyes…the green had become brighter, he swore, over the past year. For a woman so young, she had carried a lifetime of living, of hurt, of love. It was in her expression, the shadow of her eyes, always there, and those memories were the first place she went whenever something bad happened. Then she'd stop and take a breath. He saw it time and again, thankful it was happening less as the days passed and she was starting to believe that Andy would always protect her and keep everything bad from touching her and the children. If something happened, he wanted her first thought to be free of worry, knowing she was safe, believing he'd protect her and their family.

She leaned in to his touch, and she didn't have to say a word for him to know she trusted him, giving herself to him so freely to touch, to caress, to taste, and to be with whenever he needed her. She was so damn responsive to him, and he didn't think he'd ever have enough of his woman.

He kissed her neck as his hands slid under her light T-shirt, lifting it over her head and tossing it to the floor. His other hand slid up her back, over the soft skin and up her spine, and again she pressed closer to him, her hands gripping his shoulders tighter. She gasped as he unclasped her bra and divested her of it, and he stood up and laid her on her back against the glass top of his desk. She was so bewitching as he pulled away and slid her zipper down, pulling off her jeans and socks until she was naked on his desk, and then he just studied her for a second, every inch of her creamy white skin: the tiny marks across her almost flat stomach, her breasts, which had always been a generous handful but had grown a cup during her pregnancy. They were firm and large, and he savored the moments he could run his tongue over her nipples and kiss and touch every inch of her after he made love to her over and over, marking her so she knew she belonged to him. He could be gentle and rough, hurried and slow, but every time he came in her it was with her coming around him. It was a connection so strong, so powerful, and one he had never expected.

"Are you going to just stare at me, or are you going to have your way with me before the kids wake?" She raised her arms above her head and spread her legs so he could see all of her.

He said nothing as he unzipped his jeans, freeing his erection. Laura wiggled on the desk as her face flushed, maybe anticipating how he'd take her.

As he ran his hand up her thigh and then spread her wider, he took her deep and hard, forcing another squeak from her lips as he moved the way he knew she loved. Being together was instinctual as she wrapped her legs around his waist and ran her hands up his chest, clutching his shoulders and hanging on while Andy made love to her, drawing out just enough that he could send her over the edge and have her scream out his name as he filled her over and over.

Chapter Two

Andy was her rock. At one time, it had terrified her to depend on him so much. He had become the center of her world, which could be dangerous when she found herself alone again, stumbling to find her footing. It had been a hard road, learning to trust Andy. Although he was far from perfect, the fear of loving him so deeply had turned into a bone-deep terror at the idea of living a life without him. That was what Laura was worried about now.

She depended on him for everything and knew without a doubt that he'd kill with his bare hands any man who tried to hurt her or their children—even Gabriel, the illegitimate son she'd had when she was fifteen, who now had her husband's name. He might not have looked like Andy, but he was her husband's son in every way even though they didn't share the same blood. To Andy, their family meant the world, so much that he'd sacrificed everything, including his own family, for her.

She loved him for that, for the choice she'd never asked him to make.

She was holding the baby over her shoulder. Sarah was making soft gurgling noises and cooing as Laura rubbed her back. She loved the fresh baby scent and the light smattering of auburn hair on her daughter's head. Whose side she'd gotten that from, Laura wasn't sure, with her being blond and Andy a dark-haired Friessen. She rocked her baby as she watched Andy outside with the kids. Gabriel was riding the gelding Andy had bought for him. Now in the third grade, he looked so big, sitting in the saddle with a confidence that came from all the hours he'd spent with Andy on horseback. The twins were holding Andy's hands as they walked through the field, and he was laughing at something Gabriel had done.

It tugged at her heart, watching her big strong alpha male and the love he had for his children, so involved with them. He was so good with them, and they worshipped the ground he walked on. Her children would never know her worry. How could they, having a father like Andy?

She glanced at the clock, as it was approaching four and she still needed to finish dinner and set the table for Kim and Bruce, who were both coming for a visit. Kim was their neighbor on the next property down, and Bruce, her fiancé, was the family pediatrician, the man who'd saved Gabriel. For that, Laura would always be grateful. They had been down a long road to feel accepted in this community, and now they were. Their friends were a group of unlikely neighborly people who showed up, called, and potlucked often. It was a way of life she loved.

The oven dinged, and Laura settled Sarah into the baby swing, winding it so she could finish getting dinner ready. Tonight she thought she'd try something different. Along with two salads, there were roasted vegetables and a side of pork instead of the beef they ate almost every night. But then, this community was all about cattle ranching. The pork was from Mavis, a rancher who'd spent a lifetime raising pigs.

She pulled the roast from the oven. It was browned and fragrant and wouldn't need much longer. She popped it back in and turned off the heat, then took one last look in the dining room. The large square table, which seated eight, was set and ready. All she needed were the napkins, wineglasses, and cups for the kids. Large windows filled both sides of the room, bringing in light while over-looking the seventy-acre spread. She could see the long-horns Andy had raised in the distance. The odor was something she was still getting used to. Andy teased her often when he stomped up the back steps in his cowboy boots after being in the field for hours on end, saying all Laura needed was to spend time out there with him on her own horse, which she'd ridden only half a dozen times.

The problem was she was terrified of horses. Andy had bought her a gentle mount, hoping she'd be comfortable in time. One day, she would. When not pregnant and caring for his babies, she'd get back in that saddle and surprise him. It was a promise she'd made to herself.

"Kim and Bruce are here," Andy said, poking his head in the back door and sending Chelsea and Jeremy scam-pering in.

"Mama, they're here! Our dinner company's here!" Chelsea exclaimed as Jeremy kicked off his little cowboy boots, his T-shirt stained with grass.

"Andy, dinner's almost ready. I need you to cut the roast before we eat."

He smiled. "You okay with these two?"

"Yeah, I'll get them ready." She scooped the baby from the swing. "Come on, you two. Let's get you washed up." She could hear the chatter of Bruce and Kim outside and the happy greeting as the twins ran, as they always did, to the bathroom to pull out the stool and wash their hands.

"Hello!" she could hear Kim calling out from the front as the screen door squeaked.

"Bathroom, Kim!" she said. "Kids are just washing up."

Kim's footsteps echoed in the hallway, and she popped her head in. There was such warmth radiating from Kim as she tiptoed behind Jeremy and Chelsea and scooped them up, kissing their cheeks. They, of course, broke out into a fit of giggles.

"You're so good with them," Laura said as she led the way back into the living room, Kim bringing the twins with her.

"I could take these two home with me, they're so darn cute. All your beautiful children," Kim said, and it wasn't the first time Laura noticed her sadness. She had no children, but anyone could see she wanted one of her own.

"Where's Bruce?" Laura asked, though she could hear voices outside, Andy and Bruce chatting.

"He stayed with Andy. They're putting Gabriel's horse away, catching up, and doing whatever it is men do."

She was glad, considering there had been a lot of tension between Bruce and Andy. "I really was worried for a while that things would always be a little tense between them."

Kim gave her an odd look, and then Laura realized she still didn't know what Andy had done, falsifying documents for an underage bone marrow donor—her brother, Brian —to save Gabriel. It had put Bruce in a bad spot with the hospital, she thought, although he hadn't said anything. Obviously, he hadn't shared what had happened with Kim.

"You never said what happened. I asked Bruce, and he wouldn't tell me, said it was just stuff he couldn't talk about. I guessed it was something that happened when Gabriel was so sick." She didn't push any more. Maybe that was what Laura liked so much about her. She was an older woman, closer to her husband's age, more than a decade Laura's senior.

"So what can I help with?" Kim said as she followed Laura into the kitchen. The twins raced through into the family room to their box of toys, which Laura had just cleaned up.

"Here, why don't you hold Sarah while I put dinner out? It's almost done, table's set." She handed the baby to Kim, who eagerly took her, holding her over her shoulder. She seemed nervous and awkward as if she was trying to get the hang of it, and the longing was there again in her eyes.

"I see how much you want kids. I hope you and Bruce are planning some?" Laura said, taking in the way Kim shut her eyes and rocked the baby against her.

"The wedding first, and yes, I want kids. I feel as if it's a part of my life I missed."

"It's not too late, you know." Was there something else she didn't know? She wondered whether Kim would even share. Maybe she was prying.

Kim didn't say anything for the longest time as Laura pulled out a serving platter and the salads from the fridge. "I'm nearly thirty-seven, not young like you. I hope so, though," she said, appearing lost in thought.

She heard voices, Andy and Bruce, and Gabriel, too, as they came in the back door.

"Go wash up, bud. Laura, dinner ready?" Andy asked as Gabriel went to the small bathroom off the back door.

Bruce stopped at Kim, taking in a cooing Sarah and touching her soft head. It was such an intimate moment, watching the two of them together. Laura exchanged a glance with Andy as he walked up behind her, sliding his hands over her stomach and kissing her cheek. The way he always touched her like this, pulling her against him in those few seconds, was like a stamp, saying she belonged to him. It made her proud.

"I'm going to wash up, and then I'll carve the roast," he said. He walked away then, her eyes going right to his ass and the way he filled out a pair of jeans. The man was absolute eye candy, someone every woman coveted, but he was hers.

"Sarah looks good," Bruce said, shifting into pediatrician mode as Kim passed her to him.

"So where can I help?" Kim asked. She was pressed against Bruce, and she kissed his shoulder as he held the baby before looking over to Laura.

"Put these salads on the table. I'll dish up the vegetables, and then I think we're ready," she said.

Andy was back a moment later, and Laura left her very capable husband to finish carving up the side of pork while she rounded up the kids and got them seated.

LAURA WAS LAUGHING, sipping on her glass of water and leaning against Andy as they listened to Kim and Bruce talk about their upcoming wedding. Dinner had been fantastic, and Laura was turning into a really good cook. There was half-eaten food on the kids' plates, their chairs now empty, as they were the reason for the noise coming from the family room. They were deep in their toy box, with toys covering the floor, playing while the adults finished their meal and chatted.

"Oh, Laura, that was fantastic," Kim said after she had finished the red wine in her glass.

"Glad you enjoyed it," Laura said. Andy lifted the bottle of red wine and refilled his glass, topping up Kim's, too. He leaned over to fill Bruce's.

"No more for me. I have an early morning and rounds." He covered his glass with his hand, and Andy set the bottle down.

Laura still wasn't drinking. After the twins, she had finally turned the legal drinking age, but then she had been nursing, and then pregnant again with Sarah, and then once again nursing. Alcohol wasn't something she was about to try. She was such a good mother.

Andy touched the edges of her blond hair, which was longer now, hanging past her shoulders.

"It's nice to see that after four kids, the chemistry still hasn't left. Not something I see too often in my business. Moms are so exhausted, and parents shift to getting through the day and night. Suddenly, couples turn into strangers." Bruce was smiling at them.

"That's why I make sure my wife has help so she's well rested," Andy said. They had an amazing sex life, and Laura had an appetite that exceeded Andy's, keeping up with him. It was a dream—but that was no one else's business and something he wasn't about to share with his friends.

"You'll let me know if you need any help with the last-minute details of your wedding?" Laura asked.

"Yes, but there isn't much. Mom took over and is handling things. I just need to show up…"

"You kind of need me there, too," Bruce added.

"Of course, you know what I meant." Kim rolled her eyes. "*We* just need to show up. There's food, drinks, the venue. Now it's just getting to the date."

"In three weeks."

"A nice fall wedding." Kim gazed up at Bruce, who was

smiling at her. He was a handsome man, wearing rimless glasses, intense, calm—a man Andy trusted with his children.

The phone rang from the kitchen. Laura glanced his way, but he stopped her from moving, putting his hand on her shoulder and sliding back his chair. "I'll get it." He took in the kids playing and Gabriel watching TV. "You okay, bud?" he called. He wondered when the worry would pass, if ever, about Gabriel and whether the cancer would come back.

"Fine, Dad," he said, glancing at Andy and then back to the TV.

He grabbed the phone, still watching Gabriel and the twins. "Hello?" He was distracted when he heard the deep voice.

"Andy, it's your father."

He didn't say anything. It seemed as if in those few seconds, everything was more pronounced: the clock ticking, the sound of his breath, the chatter from the next room and then the kids. He rubbed the back of his head, hearing the rustle of his cropped hair. He didn't miss Laura's glance his way, and she mouthed the question "Who is it?"

He turned his back, stepped out of the room, because he couldn't let Laura know his father, a pariah, was calling. "What do you want?" he ground out, moving deeper into the living room, away, so his family couldn't hear.

"How are you, son?"

Was his dad serious? "You're phoning to see how I am? I'm great, happy. Why are you calling?" Hearing his father's voice brought an ache to his heart he thought he'd long since dealt with. Guess not.

"Andy, we've always been close. You're my son. I shouldn't have to have a reason to call you."

No, but that ship had sailed the moment his father had traded sides, using Andy as a bargaining chip for some political favor. "That's definitely a debate for another day, and one I'm not getting into now. I have friends here and a dinner we're in the middle of—"

"Andy, your mother died," Todd said, cutting him off.

"What did you say?"

There was a sigh on the other end. "Your mother was found in her room. They think she had a heart attack. She died."

"I'm sorry," he said, and he was, but not for any reason that had to do with missing his mother or loving her, because he loathed her, and maybe that was why his heart ached. He thought of the letter, the tape in the safety deposit box, the damning evidence he'd held on to to protect his wife, his children, evidence of his mother's schemes to take the twins from Laura and to get her out of Andy's life. It had been horrible. The woman had been horrible and was responsible for the death of Aida, the old cook who had befriended Laura. It was so much to deal with in that moment that he leaned against the wall.

"Thanks for letting me know," Andy said. "I'm sure this is good news for you." His father wouldn't have to be as careful with his mistresses. Hell, he could probably move one of them in.

"That's a horrible thing to say, Andy. We may have had our issues, but she was my wife."

"Yeah, I'm not really sure what that means, but as I said, I've moved on. I have a life elsewhere with my family."

"You think I don't know where you are?"

He was slipping. That was something he would have been all over at one time. His father had called him, he was talking to him now. How had he found him? He'd never told his parents where he was moving to, and he knew his cousins and uncle never would have shared that information.

"So how did you find me?"

"Wasn't that hard. You think your mother didn't know everything about where you were? She had you tracked. A detective found out everything about you in Montana. Ranching—she was horrified. How many hundreds of longhorn, that pretty little young wife, and now a new baby girl?" There was a clink of a glass in the background as if his dad was pouring a drink, dumping ice into a glass. He was listening to everything, sweating and freaking out as he looked at the open door.

"Why are you doing this? What do you want from me?" He wanted his family to go away. His mother had, after all.

"Look, I'm not calling to stir up anything. Your mother died, and plans need to be made. You need to come back. The service will be in two days. Her family's coming. Yours—"

"I'm not coming," Andy growled. "You really think I have any interest in coming back after what she did and tried to do to my wife?" He glanced up, very aware Laura was in the other room, his children playing not far from where he was. He didn't want anyone hearing, so he strode down the hall and into his office and shut the door.

"You have to come back!" his father shouted. Andy pulled the receiver away, staring at the phone.

"No, you look," he said. "I'm sorry she's dead, I'm sorry for you, but I have a family I have to think of…"

"You think I don't know that? I know you have a family. You think I haven't watched you from afar? You're my son, Andy, my only child. You're my blood, which is why you have to come. There are decisions that need to be made."

"What decisions? What does any of this have to do with me? I left, remember?" He was careful to keep his voice down. He didn't want to see fear in Laura's eyes after he swore his family would never touch her again.

"You have to come back."

"Why? Why do I have to come back?"

"Because your mother left everything to you," Todd said.

Maybe that was the cause for the uninterpretable tone he had heard in his dad's voice. As he shut his eyes, worrying about his wife, he couldn't help wondering what his mother could have been thinking.

Chapter Three

Laura was starting to wonder who had called that would have Andy this distracted and walking away from their company. That was not something he did.

"I don't know what's keeping Andy. Let me go see." Laura started to scoot her chair back.

"You know what, Laura? It's fine, stuff comes up," Kim said. "Bruce does it to me all the time, leaves me in the middle of dinner. It's hard to have people over for dinner with a doctor in the house, especially when he's on call. We really do have to go, though. Bruce has an early morning."

"It's our turn next. We'll do this again. Say goodnight to Andy for us," Bruce added as he held the chair out for Kim. "Hey, speak of the devil. There you are. We were just saying goodnight."

"Yeah, sorry about that," Andy said.

He wouldn't look at Laura, and she sensed something had upset him. He was tense, which he hadn't been in a while. The many moods of her husband. She was getting better at reading him.

Now she was distracted, watching as he shook Bruce's hand, kissed Kim on the cheek, and ran his hand through his hair the way he did when he was on edge. She followed behind him in his shadow as they walked Kim and Bruce out, said goodnight again, and then closed the door.

"So are you going to tell me who called?"

He gave her an odd look as he turned around, frowning. "It was nothing. I'll help you clean up. Then let's get the kids to bed." The swing was going back and forth in the dining room, and Sarah was sound asleep. Andy stopped and gazed down at his baby, then over to the twins and Gabriel in a way Laura hadn't seen in a while.

"I'm not a fool, Andy. I can tell something has upset you. You seem off."

"Laura, stop it," he snapped, and she must have pulled a face. It felt as if he'd slapped her. His face showed everything then as if he regretted it. He reached for her, pulled her against him. His hand pressed against the side of her head. "Sorry," he said.

She loved being held by him, but something was different. "Andy, what aren't you telling me?" She pushed away from him, and he didn't fight her. She didn't stop touching him, though, as touching him and his body gave her a better idea of what he was thinking.

"Nothing for you to worry about." His eyes took on that hooded gaze he had when he was holding on to something. He reached for her chin, and this time she stepped away, swatting at his hand.

"No, Andy, not anymore. You're not doing this to me, hiding whatever this is. I can tell you know." She stood her ground with him. At one time, she'd never have been able to. Then she crossed her arms and just waited.

"When did you become so stubborn? I find it rather sexy." He started to reach for her and pulled her to him, and she wanted to go with it. It would be so easy to be distracted.

She did slide her hands up his chest, splaying her fingers, feeling his heartbeat, his breath. "I'm still waiting. I can tell something's going on. You haven't been like this in a long time, not since…" She wanted to shiver, thinking of his mother, his family. Being away from them was a gift, and it felt now like another lifetime that she didn't want touching this one. "Your family."

"My cousins, no." He sighed and walked away as Jeremy raced toward him, latching on to his legs. He flipped him upside down and tossed him a bit. He giggled, and she loved the sound and tried her best not to smile. Maybe he knew, as he sighed. "My dad," he said, looking away and then back at her.

Her heart was hammering, and she felt her throat squeezing shut, so her hand snaked up to her neck.

Andy put Jeremy down and put both his hands to her shoulders, maybe to steady her.

"Why?" Her voice squeaked.

"My mom died."

Chapter Four

There was something about the shadows cast over the rolling hills of his land in the early morning light that made it look undisturbed. They weren't the kind of shadows filled with darkness and the end. Rather, they were filled with light and a new beginning. He almost laughed for a moment at his realization, because he wasn't someone who ever considered such things. But he'd never before contemplated life as he did now.

Now his family was everything he thought of.

He thought about protecting his children, his wife, all the while staking his claim in another state and away from the influence of his family. He loved this land, his place, his house. He loved his life, and more than anything he loved the family he'd never realized he needed.

He checked on Sarah again, then each of his children, seeing them asleep, breathing softly, safe under his roof. He stopped in the doorway of his bedroom, taking in the small huddled form breathing softly. Laura had finally fallen asleep after the tension between them. He hated seeing the look of fear in her face. She'd said nothing more as he helped her clean up, doing the dishes, bathing the kids, and settling them all in for the night. At least she'd let him hold her, and even though he picked up on her uncertainty, he could feel how much she needed him. Neither Laura nor he were the same people they once had been. She'd come a long way from the thin waif of a maid working in his mother's mansion, where he'd first laid eyes on her in that ugly sacklike dress, crouched on the floor, picking up the pieces of a shattered vase. She was now his wife, the mother of his children.

And he loved her.

Had he ever told her? He had showed her, he knew, in every touch, every kiss, every time he was buried inside of her, connected to her, closer than two could ever be. To him, it wasn't just sex. There was a fine line, and he finally understood, having crossed over to a connection so deep he swore his soul had been touched, connecting and intertwining with hers. It was on a level he would never share with anyone, and it had made him who he was now. How different his life was today, away from Caroline and away from the influence of Todd.

"Andy?" Her voice sounded so groggy as she rolled over on her side, her hair a mess as she gazed at him in the dimness of the predawn light. "Why are you up?"

What could he tell her? He hadn't been able to sleep from worrying about what he had to do and struggling with a decision he knew he had to make. "Just thinking."

She didn't say anything, but he could feel her watching him, and then she pulled back the covers without saying a word, letting him know the empty spot beside her was his.

He shouldn't, because he needed to think, to decide. "You're tired, and Sarah has been back down a few hours," he said. "She'll wake again soon to nurse. You need your sleep."

"So do you," she said again, sounding more awake.

He pulled off his T-shirt and stepped out of his jeans, wearing nothing else, and climbed in beside her. He slipped his arm around her as she curled in beside him as she always did, fitting so nicely against him. As he held her, it hit him that she was the first woman who'd ever felt so right. Her head rested on his chest, her arm across him and her leg entwined with his. He could take her right now. He was ready, he was always ready with her, and she would let him. She never denied him, and he knew she would love it as much as he would.

"Are you okay?" he finally asked her, and she sighed, running her hand over his chest, playing with his chest hair, smoothing it down and caressing him in that way she did when she was thinking.

"I should be asking you that. You've been so quiet."

Quiet, was she kidding? He felt as if his world had been rocked, and he was stumbling, wanting to protect his family, do what was right, and make sure Laura never doubted where his responsibilities lay. "I'm worried about you," he said. "I don't want you ever to have to worry again or be afraid that I'm not here for you." He pressed a kiss to the top of her head.

She turned her head and then rolled over until she propped her chin on her hand, resting on his chest, looking up at him. "You're wrong, Andy. I'm not worried about me because I know you would do anything to protect us. You moved us away, sold everything. I know you keep things from me, and there's times I'm grateful you do because I was scared to know, and scared that your mother, your family, would try to pull us apart. You're all I have, just you and our children. You're everything to me. I'm worried about you."

He frowned, because of anyone, Andy knew he could

handle anything. "Don't worry. It will be okay, but I have to go back." He hadn't decided until now. He hoped she understood.

She pressed a kiss to his chest. "I know."

He touched the top of her head, smoothing her hair again.

"So when do we leave?"

He wasn't sure he'd heard her right, and he felt cold, having to pull his hand away, resting his arm over his face and then back onto the pillow. "As much as I'd like to have you there with me, I think it would be better if you stayed here. I want you and the kids to stay."

Laura pulled away and sat up, sitting cross legged beside him. "Why would you say that, Andy? I don't understand. Your mother died. No matter what, we should be together. You shouldn't be going there alone. We're a family," she added, but this time she didn't pull away. She stayed where she was, touching him.

Andy couldn't help admiring her and seeing a strength in her he hadn't known existed. She'd been through so much in such a short amount of time. She was so young. Most her age were starting out in university, just beginning the most exciting time of their lives, experimenting with love, enjoying their freedom, and here she was, a mother of four, going from teenager to adult overnight. He wanted more for her. He didn't want anything bad to touch her again.

"We are, which is why I don't want you there. I want you and the kids to stay here, where I know you'll be safe." And his father wouldn't be lurking in the shadows. Not that he thought Todd would make a move on his wife, but he chased pretty young things, he always had, and Laura was Andy's alone. "I made a promise to you before that you would never have to go back to the estate." To his home, his mother's home. She'd never been back after the night she'd fled with Gabriel, pregnant with the twins, afraid because she'd discovered his mother had plans to get rid of her and take the babies. He felt the awful tightness in his chest return that hadn't been there for so long, a reminder of the horror his wife had felt. Worse, she had believed he could be a part of it.

"What are you thinking?" She reached up and brushed back a lock of dark hair on his forehead. "I always know when you're worried about something. You get this faraway look and seem almost angry. It used to frighten me."

He was watching her as she watched him. He knew he was intense, demanding, difficult. That was who he was, and he hadn't known he'd frightened her. He didn't like hearing that. "I didn't know that. Do I still scare you? I don't want you scared of me." The bedroom was lighter, and he was mesmerized at her beauty.

"No, you don't scare me. I learned a long time ago that everything you do has a reason. I just told myself I don't need to know when you decide something. Sometimes you tell me, and when you don't I've come to understand it's because you're scared for me, worried something will upset me. I'm so grateful that you've taken all that worry off me. Everything I've had to do alone is now replaced with you being there for me and taking care of everything, so much so that now I worry you'll take on too much and something will happen to you."

He was surprised by how sure she sounded. She'd changed so much from the young woman who was so uncertain about so many things. She'd grown into such confidence in his shadow. "I'm stronger than that, Laura. Nothing is going to happen to me." He planned to be around a long time, raising his children, a houseful of children that he'd never get tired of.

"Well, I plan to make sure of that," she said just as a cry from Sarah started in the next room. "Stay there. I'll get her." Laura climbed over him, wearing his T-shirt, which she'd slept in. It covered her rounded derriere as she walked barefoot out of the bedroom.

As Andy listened to Laura in the next room, talking in that sweet way she did to his daughter, he couldn't help thinking about what she meant. There was something in Laura that had changed her from the young woman he'd married because she needed him, his protection, his help, to this self-confident woman who had just turned the tables on him in a way he'd never expected.

Chapter Five

A car horn honked, and Laura brushed aside the kitchen curtain, seeing the city cab from Columbia Falls parked and waiting out front.

"I don't want you to go!" Gabriel said, standing in front of Andy as he said goodbye to the kids. Chelsea had her arms around Andy's neck, and Jeremy was clutching his arm as he squatted down.

"I'll be back before you know it, just a few nights. You help your mom out here. I'll call you tonight before you go to bed." He kissed the twins and pulled Gabriel to him, kissing his head and holding him before standing up and putting Chelsea down.

"Andy, you have to go," Laura said. "Your cab's here."

He just nodded, looking at the kids and then over to Sarah, who was asleep in her baby swing, going back and forth. Then he ran his hand over his mouth. She could see the anxiety all over him, oozing from him, and she also knew he needed her not to add to his worries, because whatever he was walking into, he needed all his wits about him.

He gestured her to him. Of course she didn't refuse. Her body would hate her if she tried. She walked right into his arms, her cheek pressed to his chest, and breathed him in, the sunshine, the masculine scent that had her never wanting to let go. He pressed a kiss to her head, his hand holding her to him. Then she stepped away, smiling up into the worry reflecting back at her.

"We'll be fine," she said. "Call me when you land. Let me know you're okay."

That brought a smile to his lips. He started to leave, brushing his hand over her arm, and then he surprised her when he pulled her closer and bent down, brushing his lips to hers. It was so soft and tender and so unlike the Andy who kissed her with passion, with bruising kisses meant to possess her and mark her as he often did. She reached up and touched his face, and he pulled away, his gaze connecting with hers a second or two when the horn honked again.

"Coming," he said, but she also knew the cabbie couldn't hear it. "You call Kim and Bruce if you need anything. My men will handle the cattle. Gabriel doesn't go on his horse till I get back."

Laura was holding his hand as she walked Andy to the door. This was the first time she felt as if he didn't want to let her go. Maybe that was what gave her the confidence to get him out the door. "We'll be fine," she said. "You just go and take care of what you need to, and then come back to us."

He kissed her again as Chelsea and Jeremy latched on to both her legs. Andy reached for his bag and coat resting on the front porch and started down the steps, depositing them in the backseat of the cab. He waved just as Gabriel slid his hand into hers. She lifted her hand to Andy, watching as he climbed in the front seat and then the cab pulled away.

Just watching her husband drive away had her chest tightening and her eyes tearing, so she pulled a breath to hold it together, missing him so much already.

"Why did he have to go back, Mom?" Gabriel asked. A quick glance down at her little boy, who loved Andy so much, told her he remembered everything.

"He had to, but it'll be okay. You know your dad can handle anything," she said to Gabriel as he watched the only man who'd been a father to him leave. Then he raced down the steps, waving after Andy and the cloud of dust that trailed the cab.

It would be just two days. He needed to do this, to go back and take care of his past, and then he would come home, where she'd be waiting.

"Okay, let's go in. Gabriel, don't stay out too long." She followed the twins in and lifted a sleeping Sarah from her swing, cuddling her baby, Andy's baby.

She would be okay, she knew she would, but as a shiver caressed the back of her neck, she also realized that as strong and capable as Andy was, he was walking back into the pit of the lion—and that had her holding her baby just a little bit closer.

Chapter Six

"No one would blame you for skipping out on the funeral," Jed said.

Andy's cousin had picked him up at the small airfield outside North Lakewood, where he'd grown up. He was the same height and build as Andy, tall and solid, a cousin who'd have his back. Jed was looking a little scruffy, as he always did, still wearing a ratty cowboy hat, the ends of his hair touching his ears. At times, he wondered when Diana, his wife, got him to take his hat off. He hadn't shaved, and he appeared tired.

"You okay, cuz?" Andy asked as he set his bag in the back of Jed's pickup before opening the door and climbing in. At least he'd traded in his beat-up old Chevy for a newer model with leather seats. "Nice ride."

Jed tossed him an easy smile as he started up the truck. "Diana insisted. Can't say she wasn't right. Guess I've been so used to living how I've lived, not spending much, that I've never really lived the way you have, cuz." Jed reached across and slapped Andy's chest. "Don't be worrying about me, too. Just need a good night's sleep, but not much to be had now with Mom and Dad here. They were visiting when your dad called."

What could Andy say except he was relieved his uncle Rodney was here now? He was more family than Todd and Caroline would ever be. Rodney was the father he wished he had, but he belonged to his cousins, Jed, Brad, and Neil.

"How're Laura and that new baby of yours, and when do we get to meet her? Diana's been asking."

"Anytime you want to come out and visit, I told you you're welcome, but Laura's not coming back here," Andy said. Hell would freeze over before he'd ever allow her to set foot back in this place again. It held so many memories for both them, good and bad.

"How're you holding up?" Jed asked as he pulled onto the highway.

"Fine, great. What can I say? I never expected to be back here again, or for Caroline…" He stopped talking because even though he hated his mother for all her scheming ways, he hated her more for being a cold, unfeeling bitch who saw Andy as someone she could treat as a pawn and use. She hadn't had a maternal bone in her body that could love him. That hurt more than anything.

"Not what we expected, that was for sure, hearing your mother was found dead the way she was."

Andy wasn't sure he really understood, and he looked away at the land, the acreages and forests he'd known like the back of his hand. There were trails and mountains in the distance, miles of country. "It was a heart attack, wasn't it? Found in her room, all alone. Still can't believe she went before Dad. Thought it would've been him first." He'd expected Caroline, the ice queen, to outlive all of them and keep wielding her path of destruction on some poor schmuck. Then he couldn't help feeling cheated as he thought about what was in the safety deposit box, the only evidence he had to keep his family away. He'd never known how he would use it or when. Now his chance was gone.

"No, I thought you knew. Your mom was in bed, but she wasn't alone."

He didn't know what to say, sickened when he thought of his mom and dad together. "Dad forgot to mention he was with Caroline." He let out a laugh, more of disgust than anything. "Who'd have thought—"

"It wasn't your dad, Andy. Your dad wasn't even in town," Jed said.

Had he heard him right? What he was hinting at was not something his mother would have done. "She was with another man at the estate?" He stared at Jed, who was shaking his head.

"I don't know who it was. All I know is what Dad said. She was with someone. Didn't need him to elaborate."

"Are you telling me my mom had some boy toy?" In all the years he'd been around under the same roof as his mother, she'd never entertained another man, but then, she'd spent how many months a year away in another house in another country?

"That's what Dad said. He was over at the estate with Uncle Todd."

Andy didn't know what to say, how to begin to make sense of what he was hearing. He also couldn't believe he was almost at the estate. He could see it from the highway, the vast acres, the stables, the horses, and the mansion that was like none around these parts. It had once been his home, a place that was his birthright, but one that didn't mean a damn thing anymore except a lot of memories of betrayal, anger, and deceit.

Jed parked in front, pulling up behind a black

Mercedes, a Cadillac, an SUV, and a delivery van. Andy just stared at the stone steps, the gardens, and the size of this house. It wasn't a house, though, he realized as he heard Laura's voice in his head. "She just wanted a house," he said.

"Pardon?" Jed asked.

He shook his head, not realizing he'd spoken out loud. "Just something Laura said. She wanted a home, a few bedrooms, kitchen, living room. Just a place you could sit and relax in. This place, looking at it now as she must have seen it, you could get lost in it. There were so many rooms, so many staff." He pulled on the door, and Jed just sat there.

"You're welcome to come and stay at the ranch, you know. Mom and Dad are in the loft above the barn, but we could put you on the sofa."

It was a nice thought, and he knew Laura would be happier if he did. It was only a few days, and there was something about all of this that made him need to be here to finalize things so he could get the hell out and back to his wife and children. "No, but thank you. You not coming in?"

Jed just shook his head as Andy opened the door and stepped out. "No, but Dad's here." He gestured to the house, and Andy looked up at the doorway, which was now open, the two brothers standing side by side. He shut the door and reached for his bag in the truck bed, then lifted it out and waved to Jed as he pulled away.

He took a minute to gather himself, taking in this property, this land, and the two men waiting for him. One he welcomed, the other he loathed.

He started walking.

Chapter Seven

The grand entrance was the same but different. The floor was tiled the same black and white, and as he looked up, the detail in the trim was spectacular. The grand archway into the library was eye catching, and that had been his domain for years. The deep reds hadn't changed, and he dropped his bag and coat on the leather sofa, which was in the same place in front of the fireplace. An oil painting of horses hung above the mantel, but his desk was gone, and in its place were a couple of white leather easy chairs with a large ottoman between them. It seemed emptier, different, as he scanned the room, and he realized as he looked closer that his books, his trophies, his gold box, and the bar that had held crystal decanters of liquor were all gone. It seemed as if his very existence had been removed. Everything else in the room was different.

"Your mother decided to change some things after you left. Out with the old, she said," Todd said behind him. The man was following him, his father, whom he'd once been close with. He was a stranger now. Andy glanced back, and the person he started to see was an old man who had strayed, leaving a trail of broken hearts and messes for Andy to clean up. He was glad to be gone.

Rodney was behind him, watching him and his father. The older brother, the responsible one, the uncle he wished was his father. "How was your flight, Andy?" Rodney asked. Maybe it was his way of breaking the tension that was following him.

"Good, short. So fill me in on what's going on. I need to be back home in a few days. I can't leave Laura that long."

Rodney nodded and glanced away. His father stepped closer, setting his hand on the back of the sofa. There was a bracelet on his wrist, something that hadn't been there before, a medic alert. Dare he ask?

Andy took a breath. "So…the funeral? Someone fill me in."

"Your mother's lawyer will be here shortly. Funeral is set for tomorrow, but there are some things you need to know," Todd said, taking a step toward him and setting both hands on his hips.

"You said that before. I'm curious as to what that is," Andy said. He stepped around one of the chairs, keeping his distance. Rodney was watching him and then his father.

"Your mother's family is coming. Her two brothers are here." Rodney gestured to the stairs. "They arrived last night and are leaving after the funeral."

Of course, the Kentuckians, the bluebloods he barely knew, Noah and Craig. One was a banker, the other following in his father's footsteps, running for governor. He hadn't seen them in years, since his grandfather's funeral. What had it been, fifteen years? But then, like all his mother's family, they were merely acquaintances, a reserved lot, cold like Caroline.

When he didn't answer, his father took another step,

closer, wiping his hand over his face. He seemed out of sorts, awkward, nervous, which was so unlike him. "Well, there are a few things you need to understand, and the lawyer will clarify."

Rodney was shaking his head, and Andy had a feeling he wasn't going to like what he heard.

"Maybe you could clear up the mystery now, as I'm not in the mood for twenty questions," he said. He didn't miss the way Todd glanced to his brother, and then he wondered why Rodney was even here, since he knew there wasn't much love lost between the two of them.

"Your father here found out that your mother left everything to you," Rodney said, gesturing to Todd from where he was in the archway. Before he could say anything else, there were voices in the hallway, coming from deep in the house. He looked up to see his uncles, both light haired like his mother, with the same aristocratic features, the slender noses, tall and lanky.

"Andy, my boy!" Noah was dressed in dark pants and an open-collared shirt, with cropped hair, walking in ahead of Craig, who was dressed similarly, in dark pants, a white shirt, and a sports coat. Nothing cheap about either of them.

Andy reached out and shook Noah's hand. Craig followed a little more slowly, glancing at Todd, the exchange frosty.

"Anderson, glad you could make it." Craig also shook his hand. "It's been ages. How's married life?"

It was the polite conversation he hated, knowing his mother's brothers really weren't interested in his little family. "Great. Yours?" he replied rather sharply.

"Fine. We'll be summering in Martha's Vineyard. You should join us."

What could he say to his uncles? "Yeah, sounds great."

Like hell he'd drag his family across the country to summer with a side of his family and a social scene of wealthy politicians who spent their time looking down on people like them. Laura would hate it. So would he.

"Such a sad thing, your mother passing. We never expected Caroline to go first. She was in such great health Why, we'd just seen her last month at the family home."

Ah yes, his grandfather's estate in Frankfort. This house was a replica of his mother's family home, a home his uncles still lived in with their wives and two cousins he didn't know.

The doorbell chimed through the house, and he was about to leave and answer it when he heard footsteps and noticed a maid, someone he didn't recognize, pass by. "Right," he said out loud, remembering how well staffed this house was. That was a position his wife had once been in. What a pampered life he'd had.

"Your mother said you were ranching now in Idaho, with another grandchild, too," Noah said.

"Montana," Andy corrected him, unnerved at how his mother had known about Sarah.

"Pardon?" Craig asked.

"Andy has a ranch in Montana, not Idaho, Noah," Todd asserted as if he gave a shit about what Andy did. He wondered what this fatherly thing was.

"Ah, Montana, home to the open skies and vast grass-lands, real salt-of-the-earth people."

Good God. Andy wondered how he'd have fit into this scene years ago. At one time, he could bullshit along with the best of them, but right at this moment he was more inclined to find a wall and stick his back to it just so he wouldn't find a knife shoved there. It was as if Caroline were still haunting this house.

The maid stepped into the library, her dark hair pulled

back in a ponytail, wearing that sacklike black and white dress uniform his mother insisted the staff wear. She was carrying an envelope and appeared nervous.

"What is it, Claudia?" Todd said rather brusquely.

"This just arrived for Andy Friessen." She glanced nervously over to him, and Todd reached for the envelope.

"Who's it from?" Andy stepped forward, taking the envelope from the nervous maid before his father could touch it.

"Sorry, sir, I don't know. The man at the door didn't say, just said this was for you."

Andy took in the printed lettering, his name and the estate address. Interesting. "Thank you," he said to the maid, who quickly left. He turned it over, taking in the sealed envelope, and then walked over and tucked it into the side of his bag.

"You're not going to open it?" his father asked. Of course Andy didn't miss his interest.

"Not right now." He gestured to Rodney. "You got a second?"

Andy took in his father lingering behind him and his other two uncles opening a cabinet he hadn't noticed by the wall. So that was where his mother had stashed the liquor. They were now fixing a drink, and his father walked over and joined them.

"Let's take a walk," Rodney said, looking around as if he didn't want to say too much there.

"Could use some fresh air," Andy said before looking back once at his father, whose expression was filled with something he'd never seen before: hurt. Odd, he thought.

Chapter Eight

He'd forgotten how big this property was. The flat open land, the trees and forest in the background, and miles of open trail he'd spent years exploring on horseback…he knew every part of this land up into the mountains. At one time, he'd believed he'd be there forever, knowing this property was his birthright as the only son. He'd loved this land so much he believed he'd raise his children here with his imaginary wife, and one day he would die here. He'd never imagined another way.

How everything had changed. Now, he walked side by side with his uncle to the field that corralled many of the horses he'd bought and worked with, some of the finest bloodlines around. He had been a rodeo star in his time, another lifetime.

"So how are you doing, son?" Rodney asked, leaning against the wooden rail.

"I'm good. What can I say? I didn't expect this. I'm not sure how I'm supposed to feel." How could he, considering his mother had always been so distant? He'd been raised by staff, tiptoed around his mother's theatrics. They had never been close.

"Was quite the shock to Becky and me, too," Rodney said.

"I'm surprised you're here, but I can't say I'm not happy. It was good to know you're here as a buffer with Dad. Wasn't too keen, I have to say, on coming back here after all that's happened."

"Well, the timing couldn't have been better. We came up to see our grandkids, knew I needed to be here for you. Becky insisted, too."

He didn't know what to say as he watched his uncle. His heart felt full and loved, being with him. "Thank you." His throat thickened, and he had to clear it again. "Any idea what's happening tomorrow?" He had so many questions, and he didn't know what he was going to have to deal with.

"Funeral's in the morning. Brad and Neil are coming in for it. Then your mother's lawyer is reading the will. All I know is everything is to go to you. Your dad said your mother always had it set up that way. Don't know everything, but I do know it's a lot."

"And Dad?" He didn't understand. Because his parents were married, everything should have been his dad's. Maybe there was more to it.

"I don't know everything, but you'll find out tomorrow, I'm sure. Just remember you have your life somewhere else. Your mother is gone, and so are her shenanigans."

"I never knew what to do with the evidence Aida left before she killed herself, what my mother had schemed, trying to get rid of Laura. She knew I had it, and I often wondered if she was worried about when and how I would use it. But I'm not like her. I just wanted my family safe, for no one to come in and try to destroy what I have with

Laura." He wondered now what he'd do with the safety deposit box since there would be no justice for his mother. He felt cheated in an odd way instead of relieved. At least his wife wouldn't have to worry that she'd be set up with some unspeakable crime and sent away to prison, which was what his mother had threatened. She'd had the means to make it happen, which had truly terrified him.

"Andy, you and Laura have a family, and you already know nothing can happen because we have each other's backs. Go to the funeral, listen to the lawyer, and then go home to your wife and your children. That's all you have to do. Becky and I will be here for you, too." Rodney reached over and squeezed his shoulder. "This is quite the place. You should really consider staying at Jed's."

He smiled, thinking of taking the sofa in Jed's too-small house. How much more comfortable it would be than this ten-thousand-square-foot luxury mansion. He shook his head. "No, as much as I'd like to, I can't. I'll take my old room if it's still intact and just go through some things." Mainly his mother's, her records, to try to get a handle on what was coming tomorrow. Then he'd call his wife, relieved that out of all this tension, she was hundreds of miles away in another state, safely away from all this.

"Call if you need anything." Rodney squeezed his shoulder one more time before pulling him into a hug, patting his back, and then walking away.

Andy took in the horses, the stable workers, and the cars in back from the employees of this vast estate that he'd one day expected to run. For the first time, he felt the power behind this place—unsettling.

Chapter Nine

Sitting around the table with her children, the baby on her lap, as she poked at her plate and the dinner she'd made, she couldn't help missing Andy. His spot at the head of the table was empty, a reminder he wasn't here. It was silly, this feeling she had, missing him so much, considering they were together day in and day out. For some, the break would have been welcome—but not with Andy, not for Laura.

She didn't think she'd ever tire of knowing he was there. She wished he'd call. He'd been gone all day, and although she realized on some level that he had a lot to deal with, she wanted to hear from him because he and their children were the center of her world.

"Mom, aren't you going to eat?" Gabriel asked as she stared at the chicken casserole she had moved all over her plate. She had no appetite, and to her, tonight, food was absolutely tasteless.

"Not hungry, I guess, but I will." She shoved a forkful in her mouth just so her child wouldn't worry. Gabriel had eaten half his dinner, and the twins had spilled most of theirs on the table.

"All done," Jeremy said as he pushed away, his hands a mess. Chelsea was holding her sippy cup, drinking her water, sitting nicely in her booster seat.

"Whoa, hang on a second. Let's wipe your hands and touch nothing." Laura jumped up, holding the baby, and went around the table to take Jeremy to the sink in the kitchen, where she wet a cloth with her one hand and wiped at his.

She heard a truck and glanced out the window, seeing Kim looking so confident as she started up the steps. There was a knock on the screen door.

"It's open," Laura called out, hearing it squeak.

"Hey there, I hope this isn't a bad time, but I thought I'd stop in and see if you need anything." Kim strode into the kitchen, setting her purse on the counter and flipping her sunglasses on top of her head. Her long brown hair hung in waves down her back, and she wore blue jeans and a blue checkered shirt. "Actually, I was bored. Bruce is on call at the hospital and was called in this morning for an emergency. He'll be gone all night, I'm sure. I've cleaned every inch of the house top to bottom, weeded the garden, and now that I'm done with all those mundane tasks, I hoped I could bug you for a bit."

"Glad you stopped by. Your timing is perfect. I was starting to go stir crazy," Laura said as Jeremy raced over to Kim and she lifted him, giving him a kiss. Of course he wanted down immediately and took off to his toys.

Gabriel walked in, carrying his plate, and put it on the counter. "Hi, Kim. Do you want dinner? Mom made a chicken casserole. She hasn't finished hers yet."

"Chicken casserole, that sounds good," Kim said, looking over at Laura and touching Gabriel's head. "But I already ate, thanks, Gabriel. Why don't I sit with you, and I'll hold this gorgeous sleeping baby while you eat?" Kim reached for the baby in Laura's arms.

"Mom, can I go out and brush my horse?" Gabriel asked.

"If Bert is out in the stable, then you can, but your dad didn't want you out with the horse while he's gone."

"Dad said he didn't want me to ride. He didn't say anything about brushing him," Gabriel said.

He was right, Andy hadn't said that, but she also knew Andy didn't like Gabriel or any of the kids around the horses or hanging around the barn when he wasn't around. Laura wasn't comfortable at all with the horses, and she didn't know the men he'd hired to help well. She knew Andy had already warned them to steer clear of the house and her.

"Brush only, and check with Bert first," she said and watched as Gabriel raced out the door.

"Are any of the men staying while Andy's gone?" Kim asked, peeking out the window toward the barn.

"Only Bert is," she replied. The gray-haired widower was the only one Andy felt comfortable leaving there with her.

"There he is. Good man. I remember his wife, died of cancer four years ago. He's great with horses and kids, too," Kim said, shaking her head.

"Mama, I'm done," Chelsea called out, pushing her plate away and then slipping out of her booster seat.

"Whoa, wait." Laura grabbed her before she could race to join Jeremy and quickly wiped her sticky hands and face. "Go," she said after kissing her daughter's cheek.

"Sit down, finish dinner," Kim said as she pulled out the chair where Andy always sat at the head of the table, Sarah cooing in her arms.

"I'm really not hungry." Laura sat down but pushed her plate away, resting her arm on the table. "I've been waiting for Andy to call and haven't heard from him. I'm starting to go a little crazy."

Kim was watching her and then smiled down as Sarah kicked her legs and cooed. "Maybe you should call him."

"Maybe. I just didn't want to bother him, considering everything." She didn't have a clue what Andy was walking into. She broke out into a cold sweat, thinking of him back there at the mansion, and her here.

"How come you didn't go with him? We were a little surprised when we heard his mother died and you all didn't go back," Kim said.

Of course, Kim didn't know the kind of family Andy had come from. She'd only met his cousin Neil and his wife, the kind of family that had people's backs, not the scheming, backstabbing kind that Andy had grown up with. Laura was just grateful Andy wasn't like them, because there would have been an entirely different future for both her and Andy then, one that wouldn't involve her being with him.

"Andy isn't close with his parents," Laura said. He had walked away from everything for her, for their children. "His mother wasn't a nice person."

"Oh, I never knew that. We were surprised when we heard she had died. He's never mentioned her. I just assumed a lot of things, but I know family can be complicated."

Laura thought she didn't have any idea how much.

"Why didn't you go with him?" Kim asked.

"He didn't want me there," she replied. As soon as she said it, she could tell Kim was taking it the wrong way. "Not as it sounds. He's worried and didn't want to see me hurt. You see, his mother and father had plans for him, and those never included me. Andy comes from a lot of money, and some stuff went down, and Andy made a choice to walk away from his family for us."

"He worries too much sometimes, I see, but he loves you," Kim said. "Anyone around you two can see it. You're sitting here worrying about him now, and it's so cute. Why don't you join him?" Kim skimmed her hand down the baby's arm and then kissed the ball of her foot.

"I would love to go, because I am worried. I know Andy so well. He's going to try to handle it all, and I don't want something coming out of nowhere to hurt him. I told him I wanted to come, but he insisted we stay. If you'd have asked me a year ago, even, I'd have probably said I wouldn't go back. I'd have been glad to stay here, because I would have been too scared to go."

"But not anymore?" Kim asked.

She couldn't remember when it had happened, when the fear of someone stronger and more powerful hurting her had faded. Maybe it was from being with a man as strong as Andy, living in the shelter he provided. For the first time in her life, she was safe. "No. Besides, Andy's cousin Jed and his wife, Diana, are there, and we're close, or we were…"

The phone rang, and Laura jumped up just as Kim said, "Go answer it."

Her heart was racing as she hurried to the phone. "Hello?"

"Laura."

Just hearing his voice lifted her spirits and, at the same time, brought an ache to her heart. She missed him so much. "I was starting to worry because you hadn't called. How are you? How are things there?" She pressed her hand to her chest, wishing he were here and about to walk through the door instead of a hundred miles away with a state between them.

"Sorry, I had a few things to take care of here." He chuckled. "Stop worrying. Funeral's tomorrow."

"And you'll be home after that?" He'd said two days, but she didn't want him gone longer, and there was something about his parents and the things they could pull that had her mind going places she didn't want to go. Even though his mom was now dead and she reminded herself there was no logical reason for concern, if anyone could reach beyond the grave, it would be his mother.

"A few days, I promise. I'll let you know if I need to stay longer. How are the munchkins?" He sounded so tired. She really wished she could be there to see his face and all he was trying to hide from her, rub his shoulders, his back, just touch him.

"Good. They miss you. Just had dinner, and Kim's here."

"That's good. Any problems with Bert or the men?"

"No, no. I haven't seen the others, but I know Bert is handling everything. Gabriel's out brushing his horse now."

"Laura…" Andy started, and she could hear in his voice that he wasn't happy.

She jumped in before he could finish. "Andy, I told him to ask Bert if it was all right first, and Bert is there with him." She glanced out the window then to see Bert leading Gabriel's horse outside the stable to tie him up. "I wouldn't let him otherwise."

"No riding, though," he added.

"I know, and I wouldn't let him," she said, sighing, wishing she could talk to him all night.

"I miss you guys. Give the kids a kiss for me. I'll call you tomorrow after the funeral and let you know when I'll be back." She could hear a man's voice in the background, and then Andy said, "Listen, I've got to go."

"I love you…" she said, but he'd already hung up. She just held the phone, staring out the window, feeling a wall form between them that hadn't been there before. She didn't like it.

"Everything all right?"

She hadn't heard Kim come up behind her. "He's distracted," she said. She squeezed the phone, still smarting at having been dismissed. It wasn't logical, but she wanted to come first before anything else in Andy's life. "The funeral's tomorrow. He's going to call after and let me know when he's coming home. Could be longer. I hope not."

"You should go," Kim said, but she didn't know what she was saying, considering where Andy was.

"I don't think Andy would like that," Laura said. He'd be angry, but then, she'd be with him. Even though he'd probably be really mad at first, his madness had a way of making her feel cared for, and she wanted to be there to protect him. If he knew that, he'd laugh at her.

Kim shrugged as she rocked the cooing baby. "Just saying, if it were me, I'd be on my way there. You can leave the kids with me and go yourself."

It would be easier, and she was tempted, but leaving her kids with anyone wasn't something she could do. "I'm nursing Sarah. I couldn't leave her. Besides, driving all the way there…"

"It's probably an eight-, nine-hour drive. Add a few hours in for stopping to nurse, if you left at dawn, you could be there by suppertime. The roads are good." Kim was planning it out, making it sound so simple.

She shouldn't have been doing this, and Andy would probably be furious, but it would be worth it just to be there with him, to hold his hand, to touch him, to feel him beside her when she woke. She missed that. She considered it as she pulled her lower lip between her teeth. Then she took in the kids, the twins, the baby in Kim's arms, and Gabriel, who was outside.

"You're right." She put the phone back in the cradle to let it charge. "I'm going. Would you mind staying for a bit so I can pack up tonight to be on the road early?"

Kim winked. "Go, go. I've got these guys. Whatever you need me to do, just let me know."

What would Andy think? Would he be happy, after he got past how angry he would be, that she had driven all the way there? She knew him well and at one time had worried about what he thought and how he reacted, or rather overreacted. But what she knew now and hadn't then was that everything he did, said, and worried about always came down to love. After all, he'd married her to protect her even though he hadn't loved her then, but something had happened that she'd never expected. Love had happened, sneaking up on her and him softly and quietly as if creeping in the back door until she realized how deeply and madly she loved him, and he her. Having a man like Andy Friessen love her with everything he had filled her with the powerful knowledge that whatever decision he made for them would be out of love.

Chapter Ten

Dinner had been the same four-course meal his mother had insisted on while he lived in this house. He really hadn't paid much attention to the extravagance, the dinner settings and the state of dress that was insisted on before coming to the dining room. He was the only one not wearing the required semiformal attire, instead having opted for blue jeans and a deep green Henley, which had earned him a raised eyebrow from his father and a chuckle from Craig.

There were a butler and maid who set the courses prepared for every meal, refilled glasses with wine, and cleared everything from the table. It was far different than the simple casseroles Laura often threw together. He missed the clatter and the smiles on his children's faces, the food that was smeared everywhere on the table, on their faces, and spilled onto the floor. It was a sight that would never have existed in his mother's dining room.

At the estate, children had always been banished to the kitchen, where the staff looked after them, fed them, and then ushered them off to bed so the adults could dine in peace. It wasn't until he was older and responsible enough to eat with adults that he was required to be in the dining room for dinner.

The house was now quiet after the small talk from dinner, his two uncles, Noah and Craig, and his father. Then, by some miracle, all three men excused themselves for an after-dinner brandy, disappearing into some part of the house. Andy used that time to slip away and return to his room, the bedroom of his that hadn't changed from the moment he'd packed up his and Laura's belongings after she had the twins and moved them out.

The room was the same, neat and tidy, as if it had been waiting for his return. A four-poster mahogany bed filled the center of a room richly decorated in golds and white. For the first time, he found himself looking at it through the eyes of his wife, as she had seen it. The wealth, the comfort. The plush white chairs placed just so in front of the huge mantled fireplace. The fireplace was lit as if someone had stepped into the bedroom and readied it while he ate. His bag, which he'd left on the sofa downstairs, was sitting open on the bed. He realized as he walked closer that someone had unpacked his things. The envelope, though, was sitting there with his bag, unopened.

He pulled open the large chest of drawers and saw the few items he'd packed folded neatly. The large walk-in closet was open, and he noticed his suit was hanging there alone. What was it about this room that had appealed to him at one time? He walked into the large en suite, taking in the huge walk-in shower with four sprayheads, which could accommodate an entire family. The sunken bath had jets that he couldn't remember ever using. Looking at all the splendor, the gold faucets, the comfort here, left him missing and wishing for the comfort of his home in Montana. He laughed to himself as he thought of what his wife had said, how this wasn't a home, it was a palace filled with art and useless trinkets. She had always worried that Gabriel would touch or break something worth more than the average person made in a lifetime. A home was a place he could relax in, a place that was his, where he didn't have staff catering to his every whim. How right she was.

"It's just for the night," he said to himself, wondering if he should call Laura again, feeling bad for having cut her off earlier, but as he glanced at the clock, he knew it was too late. She'd be asleep or should have been. He'd call in the morning.

There was a light tap on his door. He checked the knob, remembering the lock he knew he'd set. There was something unsettling about being in a place so big, where there were others he didn't know. It had never bothered him until now.

He was startled to see Todd standing in the doorway, still wearing his dark suit, his red and white tie loosened and the top button of his white shirt undone. His white chest hair was exposed. "Do you have a minute, son?" his dad asked.

Andy stepped back, opening the door as his father walked in. He left it open, watching Todd take in his room as if he couldn't remember what it looked like.

"Glad you came back," Todd said, then turned and placed his hand on the chair back, his gold wedding ring flashing in the light. It seemed hypocritical for a moment, this odd relationship his parents had, which he'd grown up thinking was nothing too unusual. Boy, had he been wrong.

"What's up?" he said, feeling such distance with the man who'd raised him.

"What happened to us, Andy? We were always close."

"You know what happened," he said, furious that his father didn't get how messing with his personal life was a line he shouldn't have crossed. "I'm not you. You can't tell me who to be with, to marry."

"So this is about that girl you married, the maid," Todd said, patting the back of the chair.

He couldn't remember ever wanting to hit his father. He clenched his fist but stayed where he was. "Laura is my wife, the mother of my children. You'll talk about her with respect."

His father gestured in surrender. "You surprise me, son. Your defense of her is admirable, but not sure how wise or smart it is. Women are unscrupulous when they want to be. Know how to wrap a man around their fingers and break his heart in the next. Maybe you need to learn the hard way when she strays and spreads her legs for the first slick smooth talker that comes along."

He had his father by the throat and slammed him against the wall. Something crashed beside him, but he didn't stop to look at what it was. "Don't you ever compare my wife to the trash you hooked up with. You're in a class of your own."

His father knocked his hand away, and Andy stepped back. He was surprised at his strength. Todd pulled at his jacket and ran his gaze over his son before laughing. "Wow, you fell in love with her. I don't know whether to be happy for you or pity you."

Andy looked away from his father, wondering how he could be related to a man like that. "What do you want? I can't believe you showed up at my door to take shots at my wife." He walked around the room and stopped at the fireplace, feeling its warmth, resting his arm on the mantle, picturing his wife here with him alone: Laura on her knees in front of him, taking him in her mouth. She was so sexy, and he wondered if she had any idea of the madness she could drive him to. He was sickened for a moment of his thoughts with a man like his father there.

"I thought we should have a word about your mother before tomorrow, before the lawyers come and we're sitting and listening to your mother's final decree."

"Seriously, what the hell is that about? You two were married, for God's sake…"

"We had a prenup. Everything is not as you think, so black and white."

He was staring at his dad, trying to make sense of what he was hearing, because he didn't understand why they'd had the relationship they did. Why hadn't she tossed him to the curb the first time he strayed? Why stay with him then?

"I can see you're trying to make sense of that. Well, it was what worked for us, what both of us were looking for."

Andy gestured helplessly. "To be miserable? I don't understand. Money, wealth, position, why? Or maybe I don't want to know."

"Your mother had secrets, her own reasons for being married." Todd walked around the chair and sat down, stretching out his legs as if he'd been invited.

"I don't get it. Why would you sign a prenuptial agreement, and why would anyone choose the kind of life you two had together?" Being away from this and married to Laura with the chaos of little ones underfoot had made him the happiest he'd ever been.

"It was an offer I couldn't refuse at the time. I wasn't looking for love. I'd had it once with a woman I couldn't have, but I realized it too late." He gestured again, and Andy was seeing a man he realized he didn't know. "I met your mother one summer when I was off the east coast, staying on a yacht with friends. She was there one night, a big splashy party where everybody was somebody. Caroline took over a room when she came in. She intrigued me, made me laugh like I hadn't in a long time."

"And she was wealthy," Andy added, having a hard time understanding a man who could marry a woman just for money. "You weren't broke. You had money, so I don't understand why."

"She had more, a lot more. Position, power, everything. She made things happen that the average person couldn't control. I didn't go into anything with your mother like some wet-behind-the-ears teenager. I knew the kind of family she came from. They were the kind of people who changed the world in a way average folk could only wish for. They made laws, changed them, bent them, and lived in a world they created. Besides, there was never love between me and your mother. There was a mutual under-standing, an agreement."

"You mean a business decision, something cold and sterile, drafted in a boardroom, signed and sealed." He couldn't imagine, even though he knew Caroline and Todd had wanted the same for him with the senator's daughter, Alexis. She was a nice young woman, and he often wondered how she was doing.

"Love has no business in a marriage. That's only for fools."

Andy started to say something but stopped, because how could he convince a man who was this old and should have had more wisdom and sense? His father was such a disappointment. "Well, I feel sorry for you because you're so wrong. If you think I'm a fool for loving Laura and her me, then I'm happy for it. Every morning when I wake beside the most amazing woman who has given me a houseful of children, who loves her children and is the best mother to my kids, who stays at home, raising my children, nursing my baby, I have to remind myself every time I walk in the house, into a room, that it's not a dream. When I hold my son or daughter, when they wake from a bad dream and they look to me to make everything all right, that kind of unconditional love and trust is what my family is all about, and I wouldn't trade it for anything. You can't buy that," he said, watching something in his father's expression that confused him.

"You sound like I did at one time, idealistic. I just hope you don't ever have to learn the hard way that life doesn't work that way. Don't be so quick to dismiss the arrangement your mother and I had. It wasn't all bad."

How could his father say that? Did he only know and understand one way of living? If so, how could he embrace what Andy had with Laura? "You said you had a prenup. What exactly does that mean?" His father had said his mother left everything to him, but Caroline's life had been complicated. He knew he would inherit everything, but he'd assumed it would be after his father died.

"The kind of money your mother comes from requires a contract before anyone is wed. Her father approached me, and we had a discussion about the future, as he called it. It kind of came out of the blue, considering marrying anyone was the furthest thing from my mind, but your grandfather called it a smart business move. I didn't need to love her, or her me. The only requirement was to provide an heir." He gestured to Andy.

Andy wanted to snarl in disgust. He'd always wondered why his parents had had him. He guessed he had his answer. "And here I am. So cold and clinical," he spat out.

"Everything isn't so simple, you know. The first time I laid eyes on you, you stole my heart. I loved you. I love you still, which is the only reason I did everything I could to make sure you had the future you're entitled to. You were destined for great things, Andy, and you tossed it all away for a young pretty thing. I still can't understand why you would have done it for that maid."

Maybe it was the look of murder Andy knew he was flashing back at his father that had Todd gesturing between them again. "I know you said you love her and the nice little family you have now, but you're thinking with your heart, and that's a one-way ticket to nowhere. One day you'll wake up and realize how right I was, and it will be too late."

"I don't want to hear you put down my wife or try to say she isn't good enough for me. The fact is there are days I know she was the prize, not me." He stepped away from the mantle because all this talk and the two sides of the fence they were on were making him tired, pissed, and anxious to get the hell out of this house and home to his family.

"Look, Andy, you're my son. Nothing will change that. You have a birthright you were born into. It's your bloodline. Your grandfather was the governor of Kentucky for a decade. He lived in politics, running this country. What very few know is that there are only a few families who truly make the decisions in this country, this world. Your mother's family is one of them. You're one of them. I signed that prenup understanding what I was getting into, but being part of a family that has that kind of power is something you want."

"So I don't understand what it is you're getting or not getting from all this." He gestured across the room. "Why is this not coming to you?"

Todd glanced away. "It's what I agreed to. I'm not poor, but this house, the house in the south of France, even the property in Frankfort, which Caroline shared with her brothers, is all in her name. All her assets are hers. Anything we had together had a contract. The prenup was all about money and leaves me well provided for."

"So you're saying Mother left everything to me, and you get nothing."

His father's face hardened. "There's a trust that will provide for me for a long time, but there were other things that were agreed to and must never come to light."

Now his father seemed really off. "Oh, I'm not sure I want to hear this."

"Your mother had a lover."

Todd was going to tell him, he realized, whether he wanted to know or not. "Yes, I understand that was how she died. She was with someone." He still couldn't get his head around it.

"I was a front to protect your mother's image, and if the truth were to ever get out, the trust that was left for me would disappear."

For the first time in his life, he was speechless, feeling as if he'd been flung into the middle of a comedy and he was the punchline. Maybe it was the odd expression on his father's face in that moment, but he was starting to understand what this was really about.

"So what you're telling me is that Caroline had some dark side, much like you, but no one was ever to find out, or you'll lose everything. Is that what you're trying to say?"

His father glanced to the open door, got up, and walked toward it. Andy was positive he was leaving until he heard the door close. His father was still standing there with an odd look on his face. "Your mother had a lover, the same woman for nearly thirty years."

It was one of those moments Andy wanted to laugh, but he stopped when he realized his father was dead serious. "Are you telling me my mother was gay?"

"That's exactly what I'm saying. Your grandfather

knew, and I was very generously provided for to keep her secret, but when she died here…"

"Are you saying that whoever this woman was, mother was carrying on with her here in this house?"

"She was with your mother when she died. She was the one who called me."

"So you knew her?" he said. Why was he even asking?

His father shook his head. "She was your mother's personal assistant, so it was never unusual that she was here with her."

"Delores and Mom?" he said, trying to get his head around it. He remembered the slender gray-haired woman with the bright smile, the kind eyes, a woman he'd known well and who'd been a buffer between him and his mother for years.

"There have been whispers with the staff. No one can know, Andy."

He didn't know what to say as he stared at his father, slowly understanding his meaning. Whatever happened, Andy was now holding the strings to his father's future. At one time, maybe that would have made him happy, but right now, he wanted nothing to do with any of this.

Chapter Eleven

The trees were losing their leaves on this warm fall day, and people stood in the cemetery, a sea of black surrounding the mahogany coffin that held his mother's body. It was strewn with roses, red and white, her favorites. Andy had forgotten how much she loved roses and was hit by a wave of sadness because he felt nothing for someone he should have loved.

For the entire ceremony, he watched Delores, spotting her in the back, where some of the staff lingered, crying softly. He pitied her, wondering how she could have loved a woman like his mother, wondering too if there was a side of Caroline that she had known and that Andy never would.

Listening to the minister speak about Caroline, he realized he didn't know anything about the woman who had given birth to him. She was a stranger to him, a mystery. For all the reasons Caroline had done what she'd done, he didn't understand how someone could live the way she had.

He hadn't been listening, and he realized the minister had finished as mourners started to leave. He felt a hand on his arm. His cousin Brad, tall, dark, and a little more filled out than he was. He was the oldest of Andy's generation, the one they tended to look up to, Jed and Neil's big brother.

"How you doing?" He pulled Andy into a hug, patting his back, and Andy realized how much he missed his family. This branch of the family had showed him what family really was.

"I'm good. Glad to see you. You didn't have to come, but I'm glad you did."

Neil butted in, wearing a black suit, his beard trimmed close. His dark hair was still on the longish side, wavy and covering his ears. He wondered whether his cousin was keeping this new look. "Hey, we're here for you. You heard what Mom said: No matter what, we stick together. Besides, we just want to make sure you finish up here and get back to that sweet little wife of yours and the community of kids you've started."

He shoved at Neil playfully as Jed appeared, holding Diana's hand.

"Diana, you look good," Andy said. "Jed." He shook his cousin's hand and leaned down to kiss Diana's cheek.

"Dad's over with Uncle Todd. Said to tell you," Jed said. He had an odd expression on his face. Diana looked beautiful with her creamy pale skin, bright blue eyes, and deep red hair, which was now growing out to shoulder length.

"You should come and stay with us, Andy," Diana added, glancing up at Jed.

He wanted to smile, and his heart felt full at the way they were circling him. "Appreciate it, Diana, I really do, but I don't plan on staying long. Should hopefully have nothing more to do after today and be home to Laura tomorrow." He had tried calling her when he woke, but there had been no answer. He'd expected her to call back, but she hadn't. He'd call again back at the estate. This was unlike her. Maybe he'd call Kim, get her to swing by and look in on Laura.

Diana was the only woman standing with him and his cousins, and even he noticed the looks they were getting, four strapping dudes in dark suits and their good looks. That was what Laura would have said. He smiled.

"It's too bad Laura couldn't come," Diana said. "Would've liked to have seen your new baby. Did you bring pictures?"

Andy couldn't help grinning as he pulled out his cell phone with an image of Laura holding Sarah after she'd given birth. To him, it was beautiful even though Laura's hair was a mess and she looked tired after hours of laboring. It was the one picture she didn't like shown and the one that meant more to him than all of them, maybe because it showed her love and vulnerability. "You know I just didn't want her here, in this scene, around this. She wanted to come." He held the phone out to Diana.

"Ah, she's beautiful. She looks like Laura." She showed the photo to Jed, who had his arm around her, holding her close to him. "You're too protective, Andy. Seems to be a family thing, though," she said, looking up at her husband and then over to Neil and Brad.

"No idea what you're talking about, Diana. As usual, your husband needs to keep a little tighter rein on you," Neil teased and then winked as he leaned down and kissed Diana's cheek. She patted his chest, shaking her head.

"Oh, Neil, what would we do without you?" she said.

"You coming back to the house?" Andy asked, hoping his cousins wouldn't desert him with all the high-class people he didn't know or want to know. It was a social situation he had grown up in and could manage, but he didn't want any part of it.

"Yeah, listen. Dad asked for Neil and I to ride shotgun with you. Jed and Diana will follow," Brad said, putting his hand on Andy's shoulder again. If he hadn't known before, he did now. His family had every intention of watching his back. He breathed a little easier as a thick wave of emotion touched him and he felt his throat thicken again.

"Thanks" was all he could get out as he glanced around, spotting Rodney coming his way. Todd was walking to the limo they shared on the way to the gravesite. "Where's Aunt Becky?" He frowned, looking around.

"Mom's looking after the boys. She said it would be better that way, and it was important for us to be here for you," Jed said. "You know Mom. She wants to make sure everyone's looked after, and she said a funeral wasn't a place for two high-strung kids."

Diana tapped Jed's chest. "She didn't say that. She said she could be more help staying with her grandbabies, and she loves those boys since they remind her so much of you three."

"We were never that bad," Neil said again, trying to sound serious.

"No, your mom said you were worse," Diana replied. All three of them laughed.

Rodney appeared, stopping beside Diana, putting his hand on her back. "Cavalry is leaving, time to go. Jed, Diana, I'll ride with you." He looked over at Andy, and he didn't have to say a word. Andy knew that everything he had learned last night, his uncle already knew it.

Brad put his hand on Andy's back again. "Let's go," he said, and the three of them, Neil, Andy, and Brad, started toward the limo, where his cousins had every intention of flanking him. For the first time in his life, he was happy to be who he was.

Chapter Twelve

Waking at five in the morning before the sun was up, Laura had Sarah nursed, tucked in the baby seat, and loaded along with a sleepy Gabriel, the twins, and breakfast to go in the newer Chrysler minivan that Andy had purchased before Sarah was born. With a family as large as theirs, Andy's truck just wasn't enough anymore, and Laura had finally balked at depending on Andy to drive her everywhere.

She'd been nervous at first but had found it workable, sticking in a DVD for the kids to watch for hours at a time. She'd managed to stop three times to nurse Sarah, letting the kids stretch and run before loading them back in with snacks and driving again. The only reason they were as content as young ones could be on a long drive was because she told them they were on an adventure and were going to see their daddy. It was a reminder she used a dozen times when Jeremy or Chelsea fussed, but she supposed most of the quiet manageable behavior was owed mainly to the three Disney movies she'd packed.

Sarah, though, was such an easy baby and fussed only a couple of times.

As she neared the outskirts of Arlington, closer to Andy's estate, two things began to happen. The kids had finally had enough and wanted out, and Laura began to sweat.

"Almost there, just a few more minutes and then you're going to see Daddy," she said, feeling the dampness pool under the arms of her pink short-sleeved shirt. Of all times for this to happen.

"There it is, see?" She pointed it out, and the twins started jabbering and Gabriel became quiet. She wondered how much he remembered. "Gabriel, do you remember living there?"

"Yeah. It's bigger."

It was massive, and a lot of cars filled the front driveway of the estate. For a moment, as she turned down the driveway, she questioned whether she was doing the right thing. The only problem was if she tried to turn around, she'd have a mutiny on her hands from kids who were done with this drive. Vehicles were parked all along the side of the road, and she stopped, rolling down her window as a uniformed attendant approached. She was surprised at the sense of not belonging she felt, of being way out of her league.

The young man leaned down and looked in. "Are you here for the Caroline Friessen memorial?" He glanced in and frowned as he took in the kids in back and Laura dressed so casually.

"I'm Andy Friessen's wife, and these are his children. I'm here for my husband," she said, holding her ground, fearing she'd be told to turn around and leave. Why was it that some fears of being less than others, which were so illogical and made no sense, just wouldn't go away? She swallowed the thick lump in her throat. "Can you please tell me where to park? My children have been sitting in this vehicle a really long time." She was proud of how strong she sounded.

The young man seemed to gather himself. "Of course. Sorry, ma'am. I can actually park your vehicle for you if you want to get out."

Laura shifted the van in park, turned off the engine, and got out. "Great, here's the keys. Let me just grab the kids." She slid open the back door. Gabriel climbed out first as Laura leaned in and unbuckled both Chelsea and Jeremy from their car seat and lifted them out. They both rubbed their eyes. "I want you both to hold Gabriel's hands. There are a lot of people here, and it's fancy. Touch nothing," she added, trying not to think of some priceless trinket shattering because her kids were enamored with it and just couldn't help themselves from touching it.

Sarah was starting to fuss, so Laura just lifted her out of the baby carrier, reaching for the diaper bag and feeling how wet she was.

"Let's go and get you changed. Come on, guys. Stay together and stay behind me, and let's go in and find your daddy."

On shaky legs, with her children in tow, Laura started walking to the front door.

Chapter Thirteen

It was Neil who brought him a beer, weaving through the crowd with two in each hand. He passed one to Brad, the other to Jed, and another to Andy. It was nice catching up with his cousins, the only ones who felt like family to him. They stayed beside him every time people stopped and offered their condolences on his loss, a loss he was still trying to understand.

"I appreciate you guys staying even though I know you'd rather be anywhere but here," he said.

"We're exactly where we should be, Andy, so knock it off. We're not going anywhere. We'll have some food, get you into that will reading," Jed added, tipping the bottle back and taking a drink. He held his out, and they all clinked. "Then we'll get the hell out of here."

Diana was holding a glass of club soda as she looked around. "I think you were right about keeping Laura away. I'm starting to feel like a country bumpkin here."

"I think maybe after the will's read, I might head back to your place, Jed, if you've got room."

"Yeah, you can bunk down in the barn with me, grab a

sleeping bag in a bed of hay. It will be like old times," Neil added. Andy wanted to laugh at the picture and at how uncomfortable that would be. At the same time, he knew he would probably have a better night's sleep there.

"You're not sleeping in the barn, Neil and Andy. We've got room for you. With the addition on the house and the boys in their own room, there's a spot for everyone," Diana said.

"And Danny and Christopher would insist on bunking down with you," Jed said, and they all laughed.

It would be crowded at Jed and Diana's, but at least he'd be with family he loved, those who cared for him.

Rodney, who had been shaking hands and moving through the crowd, talking to a few people he seemed to know, made his way over to Andy. "Lawyers are here. They want you in your mother's office for the reading of the will. They said just you, your dad, and Noah and Craig. It's a closed reading," he added. He seemed tense. "Up to you, son, if you want to go in alone, but I'm thinking Diana should be there, at least. Having a lawyer there for you is smart."

"My wife isn't going in there with those vultures without me," Jed said, and Diana rolled her eyes. Jed sounded just like him.

"I'd be grateful if you acted as my lawyer in there, Diana. Can understand Jed not wanting you there alone. I'd do the same with Laura." He also had a pretty good idea what was at stake for his dad, and when dealing with Caroline, he was sure there would be nothing easy or simple about this process. "I don't mind all of you hearing. Would prefer it if you were all there, and then let's get the hell out of here."

"Sounds like a plan," Neil said as they started through the crowd, nodding to everyone who offered condolences.

Brad led the way, clearing a path to Caroline's office in a glassed-off part of the house on the other side of a solarium with a small waterfall and plants. It had been her indoor garden, her sanctuary. It was peaceful.

He saw Delores at the door of the office, speaking with Noah. She wiped her eyes, nodded, and then slipped away. There was a familiar tall dark-haired man in a dark suit, with rimless glasses and clean-cut features, behind the desk. He looked up at them when they walked in.

"Andy, it's been years," he said.

How could he forget the brother of his first girlfriend, Hailey, the tall leggy blonde he had been engaged to for almost ten years before walking in on her in his foreman's bed only to learn she'd been screwing him for the past five? It was a memory he could have done without. He'd threatened to shoot the foreman, and the next day he'd learned Hailey had up and left town with him. He'd never heard from her since. *Thank God for unanswered prayers* was all he could think.

"Blair, what are you doing here?" he asked as he shook Blair Whither's hand, a firm handshake, and noticed the briefcase sitting on the desk. His uncles were already seated, and his dad stood in the back corner of the room.

"I'm your mother's lawyer, or one of them. I'm here about the will and her last requests."

He'd known Blair was off to law school, Harvard, but he hadn't known he'd come back. Last he'd heard, he was practicing in Boston. "I was told there would be lawyers," he said, seeing only Blair there.

"The senior partners are out circling the crowd, looking for business. You know sharks. They've delegated the junior associate the dirty deed," Craig added and gestured to the empty chair obviously left for Andy.

"I'll stand," Andy said.

"I see everyone is here," Blair said. "Noah, Craig, Todd…" He glanced over to Rodney, Brad, Neil, and Jed, who was holding Diana against him, and Andy saw his hesitation again.

"My family stays," he said.

The door closed. He was pretty sure Brad was standing there to block it, and at times like these, standing shoulder to shoulder with his cousins, who seemed more like his brothers, he appreciated having them in his life. For a moment, he thought Blair was going to argue, as he seemed to be considering something.

"Well, let's get on with it," he said. Smart man. Andy wondered whether he had seen the wisdom of not arguing. Maybe that was why Noah was chuckling in amusement.

Blair was behind the desk, pulling out documents from his briefcase. Andy couldn't get his stomach to unknot as he waited for whatever slap from the grave was to come from his mother. He crossed his arms and then felt a hand on his shoulder. Neil must have realized how tense he was. Rodney leaned his arm against the bookshelf.

"First off, there are a number of bequeathings to long-time staff members," Blair said.

Andy listened to the names and the amounts to be given to each of them, pocket change for his mother, but a sizeable amount for each. Then he heard Delores's name, stuck in the middle of the few longtime employees listed. He expected something more than the same pittance left to the other employees. A hundred thousand dollars, all her black heart could give. No more, no less than the others. As he looked over at his father and his uncles Craig and Noah, who had to know about the affair, it didn't seem unusual. Of course she'd be out of a job, expected to go away, expected to keep her mouth shut.

"Noah, Craig, Caroline's third interest in Larkspur, the

family estate in Frankfort, will be transferred to her son, Andy, but Caroline has stipulated conditions before the transfer of all properties takes place. Before we get to that, let's go through the list of assets."

He was barely listening, as he was stuck on the face of Caroline's lover, a woman who had faithfully stayed by his mother's side. Up until the previous night, he'd had no clue how close they had been. Neil nudged him. He glanced over to his frown. Of course, he knew Andy wasn't listening.

"Andy, there would have been documents couriered to you yesterday about the foundation and the board seat that comes with it," Blair said. "It's vast. You'll be overseeing six hundred and fifty million dollars."

Someone whistled behind him. He glanced back at Jed, who was shaking his head.

"So that was the envelope that arrived last night," Andy said. It was still unopened.

Blair kept talking, reading off the list of massive holdings, assets, all of which he'd assumed would have gone to his dad. How was he going to run all this and his ranch in Montana? This was more than he imagined. No wonder his father had paid him a visit the night before.

"Once all the conditions are met, all assets, properties, and titles will revert in their entirety to you, Andy."

He was stuck on the word "conditions" as he glanced to Neil, who was frowning. He glanced back at Diana, who appeared startled.

"Andy, what conditions?" she asked, keeping her voice low.

Andy crossed his arms again, feeling the pull of his suit jacket, and undid the button. He wanted to loosen the blue tie but thought better of it.

"Your mother owned vast corporate shares, investments overseas and domestic. She holds board seats and sits on numerous charities, all of which she's left to you, Andy, with a stipulation that they can only be left to her bloodline. Again, that will be covered at the end in her conditions."

What conditions? He wanted to shout it, but he held his tongue, wanting to raise his fist at his mother, thinking of the documents safely stashed in his safety deposit box, which he could have used if she were still alive. He wondered whether she was laughing in her grave about how she was about to outsmart him again.

"Todd Friessen has been generously provided for in his prenuptial agreement, but the agreement does not include ownership of any of the property, including the North Lakewood estate and the south of France estate, though he will continue to have access to the homes and live at the aforementioned homes as long as Andy follows the stipulated conditions.

"Todd, you will be granted an additional ten million at the end of two years if and when your son meets all the conditions set forth by Caroline in claiming all inherited assets. If her conditions are not met, you will not only lose the ten million along with the trust set up by the governor, Caroline Friessen's father, which will cease to exist at the end of two years, but all assets, cash, and properties will then be given to her brothers, Craig and Noah, and divided equally." Blair stopped and glanced up once before turning the page and continuing. Maybe he was trying to read their shock, but Andy shouldn't have been surprised at all. This was his mother's MO, and he wondered by the stony expressions on Craig's and Noah's distinguished faces whether they hadn't been entirely aware of her strategy all along. They seemed pleased. Of course they would, as they were looking to inherit extreme wealth if whatever conditions his mother set out weren't met. Or maybe they were enjoying the entertainment value of whatever Caroline's twisted mind had come up with.

Diana pinched his arm, and he glanced over his shoulder to her and didn't miss the pissed-off look on Jed's face. "Just get the conditions, and we'll talk after," she said.

He nodded again, but he really wasn't sure he wanted to hear his mother's conditions. He could only imagine what her sick, twisted mind had come up with.

"I will leave a copy of these conditions with you, Andy, along with a copy of the will, which outlines in detail the amount of the estate, all assets, and property."

Rodney stepped toward the desk in the crowded room, taking the manila envelope Blair had extracted from his briefcase. Andy wasn't sure he wanted to take it when Rodney passed it his way. Maybe he thought better of holding on to it, as he passed it back to Diana, who opened the envelope and pulled out the papers.

"Well, aren't we going to hear these conditions?" Noah said. "I'm dying to know what my dear sister has come up with to get our dear boy Andy to toe the line." He chuckled as if this was in any way funny. He seemed to think it was.

"That's entirely up to Andy," Blair said, and Diana gasped. Andy glanced back at her as she covered her mouth, reading. Jed was looking over her shoulder, obviously reading the same thing. He swore under his breath. Apparently, it was worse.

"Let's hear it," Brad growled to Blair, and Andy just nodded. He wasn't sure he wanted to.

Blair nodded and cleared his throat. "As I said, these are your mother's conditions, and if they are not met in their entirety, the entire estate will revert to her two brothers."

"Oh, and don't forget the best part. Todd, her dearly devoted husband, will be left penniless," Craig said with a laugh.

Andy couldn't look his father's way. He just waited for Blair to continue. "Here's the list of conditions that must be met: One, Andy must reside at the North Lakewood Estate as primary resident for two years. Two, only direct bloodline descendants of Caroline Friessen will reside in the residence fulltime. Any other residents will be limited to employees who live on the property in the employee residence. Three, the only exception will be Andy's father, Todd Friessen, who will continue to live at any of the aforementioned properties as long as the conditions have been met by Anderson Friessen, and he will live free of any interference from Anderson Friessen or any of his descendants. All employees and house staff will continue to report to Todd Friessen, but any hiring and firing of staff will be handled directly by an appointed guardian of the estate until Anderson Friessen has met all conditions and will assume full control.

"Four, after two years, the title will transfer to Anderson Friessen, Caroline's sole heir, for use at his discretion, and all further conditions will have been considered met and will be removed. Five, the North Lakewood property cannot be sold at any time but will transfer to Anderson Friessen's children, but only those directly descended by blood from Caroline Friessen. Six, Anderson is to take over his position as the head of Caroline Friessen's foundation, which currently employs over three hundred thousand persons. Seven, no part of the property can be sold or transferred over to any other person or family member until the two-year condition has been met. Eight, the funds to run the estate will be maintained by the law firm of

Clint Stanley and McClintock, held in trust for the period of two years from the date of my demise.

"Nine, there will be no limit on guests staying at the North Lakewood estate where Andy will be required to reside, but they shall not stay overnight in any of the listed properties for a period longer than fourteen days consecutively, and no longer than sixty days in a year. Ten, Anderson will meet regularly as set out in the attached schedule with an appointee of my choosing to ensure all the terms of the agreement are met. Eleven, lastly, if Anderson fails to live up to any of the conditions outlined in this will, he will forfeit all assets and property, which will then be relinquished to my brothers for use as they see fit. The foundation will close and be dissolved, and all employees will be terminated.

"Bitch," he heard Jed swear behind him. Diana stuffed the document back in the envelope. Andy didn't miss how tight her mouth was. He knew exactly what his mother was doing without coming right out and saying it. She was doing everything she could to find a way from the grave to rid him of Laura and Gabriel. He was sickened, thinking she would stoop so low. He heard Brad and Neil swear behind him.

"Wow, even from the grave, leave it to Caroline Friessen to try and screw you, Andy," Neil said, gripping his shoulder.

"She's still trying to have the last word, but the thing is, I don't need this or want it. I have a life somewhere else." Would it be nice to have all this for his family? Of course. Even for a moment, while he listened to those ridiculous conditions, he wondered what it would be like to have all of this, but he didn't need it. He was comfortable, not wealthy like Caroline. Even if he wasn't, he had the means to start over, but hearing he'd be responsible for that many people losing their jobs, he ached.

"You realize that in walking away, this property will be sold and you'll see nothing," Noah added.

Get out of my way, Noah, he thought, willing him to read his mind.

"Don't be so hasty, son. Your mother was being generous and wanted to see you were taken care of," Todd said from the corner. Right now, he wanted to ram his fist in his father's face at the thought that he'd even consider tossing Laura and Gabriel to the curb.

"But not my wife or Gabriel—and he is my son," Andy added. "I think not. This is bullshit. You may have lived this way under my mother's thumb all these years, but I'm out. I'm not coming back, and there's no law in the land that can make me accept these conditions."

"You're right, Andy, they can't, but I urge you to take a few days and think about it. There's a lot to walk away from, and there are many people who will lose their jobs, who will be hurt," Blair added as he deposited the documents back in his briefcase and stood up. "You should also meet with the appointee your mother arranged. Granted this is all unusual, I urge you to speak with her." He was getting ready to leave.

"She? I'm curious even though I know I shouldn't be. Who is this person my mother is dead set on putting in my path to ensure I follow her insane set of conditions?"

Blair turned, his face a mask free of emotion. "My sister, Hailey."

Chapter Fourteen

S he could hear people inside. The front door was open, and she wondered how many were here. A hundred, at least. No, maybe three hundred.

She made her way through the mourners, everyone dressed in dark colors and their Sunday best. She, of course, was in blue jeans, sneakers, and a pink top stained with breastmilk that had leaked from her swollen breasts. She knew she must have been a sight as she turned to Gabriel behind her and the twins, who were wide eyed at the decadence, the food. She warned them to behave. "Stay close to me. No running off. We're going to find Daddy. Do not let go of Gabriel's hands," she added to Chelsea and Jeremy. For once, she willed them to listen.

She didn't recognize anyone there and stopped a passing waiter carrying a tray of drinks. "Excuse me, I'm looking for my husband, Andy Friessen."

The young man appeared surprised and then glanced over her head. "I'm sorry, I don't remember who he is. I'm here with the caterer. You may want to try the regular staff," he said. Then he was gone.

"Excuse me," she said again, making her way through to the back of the house, hoping to see Andy. She could see the kitchen door and could easily pop in and ask, remembering when she worked here. She could feel the looks directed her way and even an odd expression on one man's face, as if she'd taken a wrong turn.

She made her way into the crowded dining room, glancing back to make sure the kids were still there. Sarah was rubbing her eyes and starting to fuss in her arms. Where was Andy? "Excuse me," she said to a well-dressed woman filling a plate, her dark hair pulled back in a high bun.

"Yes?" she said, smiling, before she looked at Laura. Of course, she now frowned.

"I'm looking for my husband, if you could just point me in the direction of where he is?" She juggled a fussy Sarah, who was now shoving her fist in her mouth. If she didn't find a quiet spot out of the way soon and nurse her, she was going to let out a howl. If she was stressed now, she'd really be stressed then, considering the crowd she was in.

"Who is your husband?" The woman glanced at her kids and smiled again.

"Andy Friessen," she said, taking in the woman's surprise.

"You're Andy Friessen's wife?" She looked at the kids behind her again. "These are his children?"

"Yes, these are his children and I'm his wife. Can you point me in the direction of where he is?"

The woman looked over her shoulder and then gestured to the other end of the house. "I believe I saw him head to Caroline's office with a horde of good-looking men. Oh, Jason, this is Andy Friessen's wife," the woman said to an older man, clean cut, in a dark suit and glasses.

"Oh," he said.

"Jason is my husband and one of the family lawyers."

Great! Laura felt her hand tightening around her baby. She didn't recognize the man, and he was looking around and then said, "They're reading the will now in Caroline's office. Shouldn't be much longer. Could we get you a drink or something to eat while you're waiting?" He seemed friendly, but Laura didn't like how she was being told to wait for her husband.

"You know what? I know where the office is. I'll just make my way there. Thank you," she said, turning away, hearing the man try to stop her as she moved through the crowd.

"Gabriel, Chelsea, Jeremy, let's go. Daddy is this way." She stepped into the solarium, and only a few people lingered by a door at the other end. She realized it was open, and there was a woman there: thin, tall, and leggy, in a black skirt and jacket, black pumps that accentuated her long legs. Andy was there, speaking with her, and she could see the room was packed. She could see Neil and Brad through the glass, and the minute Neil noticed her, his eyebrows went up and he slipped past the woman. He looked so good, a welcome sight. She felt relieved.

"I didn't know you were coming!" He gestured to the twins and Gabriel. "Hey, you guys, come here. Give me a hug." He picked up both Chelsea and Jeremy in both arms, hugging them.

"Where's Daddy?" Chelsea asked, and Jeremy piped in, "We drove a long time to find Daddy."

"I bet you did," Neil said. "Gabriel, you look good, bud. Get over here. My hands are kind of full with these two munchkins." He set the twins down and pulled Gabriel into a big hug, glancing over his head to Laura and Sarah, who was really fussing now.

"Sorry, I need to change her and feed her. She's really going to get loud in a minute." She glanced over her shoulder, hearing voices, and Brad called out to the twins and Gabriel.

"Laura, what the hell are you doing here?" Andy was coming toward her along with Jed, Diana, Rodney, and three men she'd never seen before.

"I came for you. I didn't want you to be alone," she said. It sounded really stupid as she looked around at the family here supporting him. Maybe he didn't need her. She was feeling really out of place.

"Did you drive all the way here with the kids?" Why was he reprimanding her in front of everyone? She could feel the stares, and she was embarrassed.

"Yes, and I need to change Sarah. Is there someplace I can nurse?" She was looking around for a corner somewhere.

"Andy, go get Laura settled," Brad said. "Hey, I bet you guys are hungry!" Brad lifted Chelsea over his head, setting her on his shoulders. She giggled. "Laura, good to see you, and is this the baby?"

Then everyone was there. Diana slipped her arm around Laura's shoulders and kissed her cheek, touching the baby.

"Andy, who is this?" the woman in the doorway said. She was standing beside him. She had long blond hair and big bold eyes, with the looks and body of a model. Laura felt her fingers tighten around Sarah, and for a minute her claws came out along with a jealousy she hadn't felt in a long time. It was ridiculous, really.

"This is my wife, Laura."

The woman mouthed a big O and then took a breath. "I see. You do realize that under the terms of the agreement, she will not be allowed to reside here with you."

In that moment, two things happened: Laura felt the ground tilt beneath her feet, and the baby started howling.

Chapter Fifteen

Everything happened so fast. Laura turned whiter than he'd ever seen, as if the blood had drained from her face, and he wasn't sure who yelled, but between Brad and Neil, one took the baby and the other Laura. He heard Gabriel cry out, and the twins burst into tears. The scene was drawing a lot of attention.

He was still trying to make sense of all this, having Hailey walk in, asserting her position as the guardian appointee Andy was to report to. Before he'd even had a chance to register his outrage, Laura had been there with his children. He was reeling, furious, mainly, because he was thinking of a hundred horrible scenarios of something happening to them after hearing she had driven all the way from Montana. They could have been killed or worse, and he shuddered to think of it. Instead of kissing her and holding her as he should have, he acted like an ass.

"Give her to me," he said, lifting Laura in his arms. She was so limp, and then she started to move, blinking, lifting her arms. "Stay still," he growled.

"Andy, we still need to speak and go over the terms of

the——" Hailey was on his heels, and that was about the last thing she should have been doing right now. He wanted to throttle her for saying what she had to Laura. It had been cruel and hurtful.

"Go away," he barked to her, and then Jed was there, stepping in front of her, ushering her away.

"We've got the kids," Brad said.

"I'm right behind you with the baby," Neil said. "Where to?"

"Upstairs, to my room," he said just as his father came out of the room, and he didn't miss the moment he saw Laura and she him. Her fingers tightened around him, and he could feel her tremble.

"Andy, put me down. I can walk."

"Like hell," he said, making his way through the crowd to the stairs, moving up, carrying Laura, who pressed her face to his chest, her arms linked around his neck. Sarah was now wailing. "Neil." He gestured with his head to his closed door. Neil went in first, and Andy put Laura right on the bed. "Sit there," he said when she started to get up.

The door closed behind him, and Neil put a diaper bag on the bed. "She's wet. You want to change her?"

"I will," Andy said, reaching for his daughter as Neil rifled through the bag and pulled out a disposable diaper. He kissed Sarah, who was becoming frantic, and pulled off her wet sleeper and diaper before slipping the dry one on.

"She's hungry. I'll take her," Laura said, still sitting where he'd deposited her. He didn't miss the amusement on Neil's face.

"So you drove from Montana with this herd all alone?" He was shaking his head.

She shrugged. "They were good. I wasn't sure I could do it. Only had to stop a few times." She shrugged again as she took the baby from Andy, reaching under her shirt to unlatch her bra, and Sarah started sucking.

Neil looked away and then started toward the door. "Andy, do you want me to see if there's a doctor downstairs in that crowd?"

He glanced back at Laura, who was looking better, but she had scared him when she keeled over. "Yes."

"I don't need a doctor," Laura said, but thankfully Neil didn't listen to her as he opened the door. "Neil, are you coming back?" Laura called out. Andy couldn't believe it. Maybe she knew how pissed off he was. It had been a long time since he'd felt this edgy side of himself.

Neil was standing by the door, grinning. "I'm finding a doctor, but you're on your own with your husband. I wouldn't want to be you right now." Then he glanced to Andy and raised his eyebrows.

"Go," Andy said. "Laura will be safe enough, but by the time I'm through with her, she won't do it again." He picked up the soaked diaper and tossed it in the trash in the bathroom. When he came back, Laura had moved the baby to the other side. She was reaching across the bed for the diaper bag and gave up when she saw him.

"There's another dry sleeper in there," she said.

Andy pulled it out but didn't give it to her. "Do you have any idea what could have happened to you and the kids? Laura, what if you had a flat tire, the vehicle broke down, or, God forbid, you got into an accident?" He paced the foot of the bed and could feel her watching him.

"We didn't get in an accident, Andy. We arrived safe and sound. Everyone's okay," she said, and he wanted to put his hands on her and shake her, to put the fear in her that was making him act so irrationally.

"You fainted downstairs. What if that had happened when you were driving with the kids? Good God, Laura, you could have all been killed!" he yelled at her, and the baby started crying, slipping off her breast.

She glanced down at Sarah, soothed her, and put her on the bed, where she kicked her legs and smiled brightly at Andy. Laura fastened her bra and pulled her shirt down, and he realized how tired she looked. He sat down on the bed, running his hand over his daughter's tummy and then looking over at Laura, who was sitting cross legged, watching him.

"Why did you come?" he said. "I told you to stay home." He didn't want her here, caught up in any of this.

"I'm your wife, Andy. I should be here with you. When you called, you were distracted. I was worried." She wasn't going to back down. "What did that woman mean about me not being able to live with you?"

Out of all of this, what ached was the fact that Laura had heard what Hailey said. "It's nothing, just some sick, twisted shit. Don't worry about it."

There was a knock on the door.

"Yes?" Andy called out, and the door opened.

"Hey, I found a doctor and dragged him up here." Neil walked in with a shorter light-haired man, who wore glasses and had a round face. "This is Doctor Grayson," he said.

"Pleasure, Mr. Friessen. I was your mother's doctor. So sorry for your loss."

Of all doctors, did he have to drag up his mother's? Maybe Neil realized his mistake, as he said in the next breath, "The only one here. Brad suggested we scoop Laura up and take her to the hospital."

"Andy, Neil, I don't need a doctor. I'm fine," Laura said, her hands folded in her lap.

But the doctor didn't seem to mind as he walked around Andy and stood at the bedside, looking down at

Laura. "May I?" He gestured to her arm, and, being as polite as she was, she lifted her hand.

"I'm fine, really."

"You fainted, Laura, keeled over, and your face lost all color," Andy said.

Neil was standing at the end of the bed, his hand resting on the post. "Laura, you scared the hell out of your husband, out of all of us. Humor us with the doctor."

The doctor was holding Laura's wrist and staring at his watch. "A little fast, but considering the commotion, I'm not surprised. Color looks good." He was looking at Laura's face and then her eyes.

"Laura, this doctor says one word about you needing to go to the hospital, and we're going." Andy wasn't sure he trusted this doctor anyway, and he was of a mind to scoop Laura up and drive to the hospital himself.

"Your husband's a little worried. What happened?" the doctor asked, holding her hands and looking at her fingertips.

"Look, I just drove here from Montana with the kids. We've been on the road since five this morning. I'm tired, the kids are cranky, and I felt as if the rug was pulled out from under me, hearing some woman say I can't be with my husband. I don't faint. I was surprised. Maybe I'm hungry, as I've only snacked on the road." She sounded irritated and hurt, and he didn't like hearing that.

"Can't say I'm overly concerned, here," the doctor said. "You've got a new baby, and that's a long drive. I'm sure with a good night's sleep, with some dinner and liquids, you should be fine. It would be a good idea, though, to eliminate stress." The doctor stepped back.

"So no hospital?" Andy asked, thinking it might have been an idea just to get Laura out from under the toxicity that seemed to ooze from this roof.

"No, only if you feel dizzy or lightheaded, head on in to emergency and get them to check her out."

There was another knock on the door, and this time Neil walked over and opened it.

Diana stuck her head in. "Hey, how are you? You scared us downstairs." She made her way in, and Jed was behind her.

The doctor was talking to Neil by the door and shook his hand before stepping out.

"Well, that was a little bit of excitement I think we could do without now," Jed said as he stopped at the foot of the bed, where Andy was standing, watching Diana holding his baby girl and fussing over Laura. He'd forgotten how close they were as they hugged, and then Diana's face lit up as she held the baby.

"Hey, so this is where everyone disappeared to," Brad said as he walked in, carrying Chelsea.

Jeremy was running. "Daddy!" he screeched as he raced to Andy, grabbing his leg. Andy grabbed Jeremy and hugged him. Chelsea followed as soon as Brad put her down, and he lifted her in his other arm.

"Oh, man, I missed you guys," he said. They giggled.

"Party's moved up into Andy's bedroom," Neil said, about to shut the door when there was another tap.

"Laura, you okay?" Rodney poked his head in, holding Gabriel's hand, and Andy noticed Todd was with them.

"Dad, are we staying here?" Gabriel asked, now pulling on his jacket. He looked worried. Brad had his hands on Gabriel's shoulders, holding him.

"Hey, don't you worry. I'll figure out where we're going to stay," Andy said.

Rodney was now standing over Diana and Laura, talking to them and Neil.

"We're too many now to crowd in on you, Jed," Andy said.

"Absolutely not, Andy," Diana said. "You already said you were coming to stay, and now with the kids, even better. It'll be like Christmas. Besides, I want some time with this gorgeous baby." Diana was fussing over his baby daughter, and Jed bent down and picked up Gabriel.

"You're not too big to pick up. What do you say you come and stay with us?"

Maybe it was his family, Brad, Jed, and Neil, settling his kids and the way they had come in here to help him fix this mess, that made him feel better. Even Laura was smiling, the baby was cooing, and the twins were giggling.

"So these are my grandchildren," Todd said, taking in the kids, looking past Gabriel to the twins, to the baby Rodney was now holding.

Everyone in the room went silent.

Chapter Sixteen

There was one thing about Andy's family: It had two very different sides. There were his cousins and uncle who made her feel as if she truly belonged to something bigger and better than anything she could have ever imagined—and then there was Todd, Andy's father, a man with a roaming eye and a fucker of anything in the female gender. As long as they were young and pretty, he considered every one of them fair game. She remembered the days working there as a maid and the number of times she'd felt her skin crawl and looked back only to see Todd watching her.

She had always made herself scarce, careful never to be alone with him, and having him in Andy's bedroom, the room she had shared with Andy for a short time, watching her children as if he had some claim to them, sickened her.

Maybe Diana had some idea of it, from the shock she knew had been plastered on her face. She could feel it in the pit of her stomach, absolutely nauseous. Andy had snapped at his father and asked him to leave. Brad and Neil had circled the twins and Gabriel while Rodney saw to it that he left. It had been quick, hurried, and the next she knew, everyone had left with the children and the baby, leaving Laura alone in the bedroom with Andy.

She pressed her hand to her chest as she breathed a sigh and then slipped off the bed as the door closed. The man staring back at her now was anything but friendly.

"They're taking the kids back to Diana and Jed's," he said, pressing the lock on the door so no one would walk in, and to keep her in. He didn't move. What he did do, though, was loosen his tie and undo the top button. Then he stepped away from the door.

"So we should go, too," she said as Andy took another step toward her, watching her with his dark eyes, the hazel that had been filled with such passion and emotion moments ago. It was the kind of fire that overcame Andy when he was unpredictable, and it always had her wanting to soften to him.

He just shook his head before pulling his tie from around his neck as he stepped closer to her and then tossed it on the bed. She glanced down to where his suit jacket was tossed over the padded bench at the foot of the bed. He unsnapped his cufflinks, and her hand pressed to her chest and her heart, which had kicked up a beat. He tossed the cufflinks onto the jacket, and his shirt soon followed.

Andy was an attractive man and solidly built. When he was dressed, he had women stopping and smiling as they took a second look, but Andy without a shirt made Laura lose her ability to reason or form a coherent thought. As she took in his six-pack abs, his solid chest with muscles and pecs that her fingers itched to touch, she knew what he could do with his strength to her when he had her under him. She knew the feel of that wall of steel pressed against her breasts, holding her to him.

She swallowed as he reached for her chin, lifting it until

she was looking into his eyes. She always knew the moment there was no turning Andy back from what he was about to do to her. She swallowed again as he ran his thumb over her lower lip, staring at the pink and then leaning down. He took her lower lip between his teeth gently, tugging so she knew exactly what he was going to do. She didn't know how he was going to take her, but she knew that he had every intention of marking her so she knew without a doubt whom she belonged to. She couldn't have pushed him away if she wanted to, because her damn body was already pushing toward him, reaching out and begging him to touch her. She nearly whimpered when he let her lip go, and he tilted his head, watching her, so much the way a predator watched his prey that her heart skipped a beat again.

"Get undressed," he said, soft and low but demanding she do it that second.

She lifted off her shirt and unfastened her bra, dumping it on the floor. Andy just crossed his arms and watched her as she kicked off her sneakers and slipped out of her jeans, stepping out of her underwear until she stood naked before him.

"Get on the bed," he said, again in the same low, commanding voice.

And she did, lying down on her back, raising her arms above her head, willing him to join her. She was trembling in anticipation, wondering what it would be like this time, hard and fast, demanding, but without a doubt she knew she'd be screaming his name by the time he was done with her.

He watched her as he kicked off his shoes and slipped out of the rest of his clothes, and then he reached for her ankles, gripping them with his hands, and pulled her to the edge until her bottom was there, and he pushed open her legs, his hands on her feet, spreading her wide.

She lifted her hips, circling, begging that he'd end her misery and take her now, but he just smiled at her and said, "This is mine. Any doubt in your head who you belong to?" But it wasn't a question. He was marking her with his words.

She couldn't get her tongue to move, so she shook her head, and then he flipped her over on her stomach, her legs dangling over the edge of the bed, and he was behind her. He entered her from behind, pressing his chest into her back, his hands holding hers high above her head. Her cheek was pressing into the mattress, and he took both her wrists in one hand, holding her so she couldn't move, and latched his other arm around her waist, holding her tight as he spread her legs wider and took her in long, hard strokes, slow and deep, with enough force he took her breath away.

He pulled at her earlobe between his teeth. "Too hard?" he asked, and she hoped he'd never worry that he'd hurt her.

"No." She gasped. "Don't stop."

She squeaked when he began to move faster, and she couldn't hold herself back. She couldn't move, knowing she was going to scream when he sank deep inside her, leaving his mark, his seed. It was a part of him she needed, she wanted, and it made her feel as if she truly belonged to and was a part of him. She was still coming apart around him, and she heard her voice crying out. She couldn't stop herself from screaming as he stayed deep inside her. It seemed to go on forever. Her legs were shaking.

Making love with Andy was the most exciting, erotic experience of her life. He absolutely, overwhelmingly possessed her, and she had no doubt of the position she had in his life.

"Again," he said, and she knew by the way Andy was thickening that she would be walking out of this room on legs weak and tired and trembling, but she didn't care, because being loved by Andy was worth everything.

Chapter Seventeen

He was almost ashamed of himself as he pulled on his jeans, his hair still damp from the shower he'd shared with Laura, where he'd taken her again the last time against the shower wall. He was acting as if he hadn't had sex in years. It was what she did to him. She made him feel younger, alive, and crazed all at the same time. She was so damn responsive and creative, and she took their sex life to a level that he didn't think he'd ever get tired of. She was beautiful, and she stirred his passion, and at times like this he wanted to mark her so every man around knew she was taken. She was his.

"Are we going to Jed and Diana's now, or are you going to throw me back on this bed and screw my brains out again?" Laura was standing by the bed, a towel tucked around her, and he could see the humor in the tiny sparks that were her amazing green eyes. They glittered now like those of a woman well loved, and then she sat on the edge of the mattress, and he didn't miss her wince.

"Sore?" he asked as she stood up and walked right up against him.

"Hmm, a good sore. I think that was a record for you." She kissed his chest, and he could feel himself stirring again. *Down, boy.*

"I was too rough, wasn't I?" he said, remembering how he'd hammered into her, holding her down on the bed, taking her from behind on all fours, then against the wall and then in the shower. He'd didn't know what had come over him.

She rubbed her cheek against his chest. "Mmm, no way, but I may not be walking straight if you want me again." She rested her chin on his chest, gazing up at him.

"You know I'd carry you out."

"You could, but I'd rather not have your cousins knowing what we've been doing when I'm a little sore to sit."

"Hate to tell you this, babe, but what I did is exactly what they'd have done with their wives—and they already know."

She stepped away, her cheeks pinkening up. "Are you kidding?"

He shook his head. "Let's just say it's a guy thing."

"A guy thing in what way?"

She really was naive. "Marking my territory." He unwrapped her towel, pulling it away until she stood naked in front of him. "Better," he said as he walked away and opened his drawer to pull out a T-shirt. He shrugged it on over his head.

"I'm confused. Did you really say 'marking your territory'?"

Andy reached for another T-shirt in his drawer and handed it to Laura. She pulled it over her head, lifting her wet hair. His shirt draped loosely over her shoulders and past her thighs. He loved it when she wore his shirts. "Yeah, I did," he said, striding toward her, feeling far more relaxed than he had in days. He leaned down and kissed her. "Get dressed. We've got to go."

She didn't move, and he could tell she was trying to understand what he was saying.

"Andy, you make it sound so…"

"Animalistic? Is that what you were going to say?"

She was nodding. "Yeah."

"It is. There's nothing civilized about what I did with you, and your response." He took in her curves, hidden by his T-shirt, and her slender legs, which had been wrapped around his waist moments ago.

Laura smiled, twisting her lips, walking over to her clothes on the floor and stepping into her underwear.

"It's kind of like keeping you barefoot and pregnant."

He had expected a reaction, but her eyes were blazing when she turned around. "What?" she snapped.

"It's a guy thing, honey. Most won't admit it, but I damn well will, because this"—he gestured from the bed to her—"is me marking you, making you mine, staking my claim so you and everyone understand clearly what is mine. And that's you, baby, my children, and the babies we're still yet to have."

"Babies? More?" she squeaked, and it was so damn cute. Didn't she have any idea he wanted a house full of kids with her? He'd never experienced the power of this kind of love. "Andy, you can't say things like that. It's not civilized."

He wondered if she was serious. "I won't apologize for who I am or for saying it. This is our life together. Are you saying it's not what you want? This is me, this way. I'm not changing."

There was one thing Andy knew: The body never lied, and Laura was downright possessive and territorial. He'd been with his wife, he knew she loved it, but as controlling as he'd been, what she didn't realize was that she had all the power. It was in her looks, her kisses, her touch, the way she seduced him and woke him in the morning, the way she spoke.

He wasn't sure what she was considering or thinking for a moment as he stepped toward her.

"Does it make me sound awful to want everything we have? I wouldn't change anything," she said, and he pulled her into his arms, her hands resting on his chest. "But you can't go around saying 'barefoot and pregnant.'"

He leaned down and kissed her. "Yeah I can, because you have no idea how sexy you are when you're pregnant with my child, when you're barefoot, walking to me like you are now. I want to lock the door and never let you out. I could drown in you and spend a lifetime doing it."

Her face flushed, and she pressed her hands to his cheeks, standing on her tiptoes as she pressed her lips to his. "Okay," she breathed out, and she kissed him again.

Chapter Eighteen

Andy had his bag over his shoulder as he led her out of the bedroom. He was holding her hand as they walked side by side down the stairs, dressed the same in blue jeans and T-shirts, a sharp contrast to the mourners who still lingered, chatting, in the foyer. It seemed as if most had left, but there was something about being well loved by her husband that erased any doubts that seemed to be part of this place and sated the green-eyed monster, tucking her back away to her safe cocoon. Andy was the kind of man who wouldn't toss her aside or stray or do any of those awful things that at one time she had worried about.

"Andy, Hailey was looking for you, and she needs to speak with you," Todd said. He was at the bottom of the stairs, and she didn't like the way he glanced her way. Of course he noticed her wet hair combed back and Andy's, too. Everyone had to know what they had been doing.

Maybe Andy understood her worry, as he squeezed her hand and pulled her closer behind him. "Not interested," he said as he stepped around his father.

"Hey." Todd grabbed Laura's arm, and Andy swung around, pinning his father against the wall, putting Laura behind him.

"Keep your hands off my wife," he snarled. There were gasps behind them from those taking in the scene.

"I got it, Andy. Sorry," Todd said. "Can we talk for a second? Just give me a minute."

Andy let him go. Laura touched his arm, holding him, feeling the strength pulse through him and the anger flexing his muscles. She'd never felt so safe as in that moment, either. It was clear then what he'd meant about marking his territory.

"Andy," she urged him, her voice sounding so strong and reasonable. He glanced back at her, and there it was again, that look he had for her. She linked her fingers with his, feeling his ring on his finger, telling everyone he was hers. The ring had been a long time coming, considering the man wouldn't wear them.

He just nodded and stepped back with her then, slinging his arm around her shoulder until she was nestled against him. She slid her hand into his back pocket as he kissed the top of her head.

"Andy, wait."

She heard heels clicking on the floor, the soft female voice of the blonde who'd made her feel as if she didn't belong.

Andy was holding her close as he turned and faced the woman. "Hailey, I'm leaving."

The tall, leggy blonde stared at Laura for a second before smiling back at Andy. It was unsettling, the way she stared at her husband. What was it about some women who thought they had a claim on her man? "I just need a moment for us to talk. Maybe we could go into the library to review some of the conditions of the agreement. I'm

Hailey, and I'm sorry we didn't get a chance to meet earlier." She held out her hand to Laura. She was bossy.

"Laura, I'm Andy's wife. What conditions?" She shook Hailey's hand because rude just wasn't something she could do.

"Nothing—and we're leaving," Andy said, his tone anything but friendly, as he moved with his hand around Laura's waist, but Hailey hurried to the front door, trying to block it so he couldn't leave. Even Laura wanted to warn her that wasn't a smart thing to do.

"Andy, it's not nothing. I feel badly your mother insisted I be the guardian. I told her it would be awkward, considering how long we were engaged."

Engaged! Oops, that ugly green-eyed monster was back, and Laura wanted to scratch Hailey's eyes out. Andy was squeezing her tighter, and maybe he could feel the moment she was about to go ballistic. She needed air and felt as if everyone was staring. She hated that feeling.

"This isn't even a discussion, so get out of our way," Andy said in warning. Laura wondered for a minute whether he was going to physically move her.

"Look, you need to talk to Andy, to get him to see reason," Hailey said, turning to Laura and actually stepping toward her.

That was when Andy put his hand out and actually moved her aside, pulling open the front door and ushering Laura out, but Hailey was dogging their heels much like one of those yappy little dogs. Her heels clicked behind them on the stone, and worse, she was talking to Laura still.

"He has so much to gain, and your children, too. This is their birthright. The estate, the properties, the foundation, the empire they'll manage one day. It's sizeable, a privilege, the kind of power you just don't toss away."

She was getting louder, and Laura could feel how tense Andy was. As she watched him with a thousand questions going through her mind, she couldn't figure out what to ask first.

"Go away, Hailey. Do not talk to my wife," Andy warned her again, and even Laura picked up the iciness in his voice as they continued down the stone steps to where several vehicles were parked.

"Andy, if you'd stop and listen, I wouldn't be talking to your wife, but this is important. Laura, talk to him. Make him understand he can't give this up. It would be foolish. The conditions only apply for two years. He's not thinking rationally. I'm only here to make sure the conditions are met. You need to make him understand it's only two years of his life. You can still see him…"

"What are you talking about?" she shouted, and she yanked her hand from Andy, wheeling around on Hailey, who was on the step behind her. Hailey stopped and jumped back. Maybe she thought Laura was going to knock her down. For some reason, it sunk in how attractive Hailey was, tall and slender, even how she was dressed, all class, a gold chain dangling over her white blouse, pulled tight over curvy breasts.

"I'm talking about the will and the entire estate of Caroline Friessen. It was left to Andy, but conditions were set out in the will that must be met before the transfer of all assets and property."

Andy was beside Laura, his hand around her hip, holding her close to him, his gaze latching on to Hailey, filled with something way past the warning he'd given her moments ago. She'd seen that look he had now, the way he was staring at this woman with fury, with nothing that said he had any feeling for her. Laura wanted answers, but this Hailey was pushing her husband into a corner, which wasn't smart. For the first time, with the way Andy held Laura to him and glared back at Hailey, she wondered whether he could hurt a woman.

"Go away now, Hailey. Walk away from me, because you have to be smart enough to know you're messing with what's mine, and you don't mess with that." The way he said it had Hailey taking a step back and stumbling. She swallowed, and the expression on her face proved she was now understanding she couldn't reason with Andy. She held up her hands.

"Tomorrow, Andy. Let's speak tomorrow after you've had time to think about this clearly and see the wisdom. I can help you. Laura, talk to him tonight," she was calling out as Andy led Laura down to a truck she didn't recognize and opened the passenger door.

Hailey was still standing there, watching her, gesturing helplessly at Andy. "Andy!" she shouted at him, but he didn't turn around as he slid behind the wheel.

"Put your seat belt on," he said as he put the truck in gear and drove away.

Chapter Nineteen

"So she was your fiancée?"

Out of that fucked-up exit, that was what Laura was latching on to?

"Was, past tense. I married you," he added as he drove down the darkened highway, putting as many miles as he could between the estate and Jed's place, which was going to be crowded, chaotic, and the only place that felt like home.

He glanced over at Laura, who appeared angry, as if she were running through a mental list of what she needed to address and what she should be more mad about.

"You married me out of obligation because you felt responsible for the mess that happened. I knew then you didn't love me."

"Fuck!" He slammed on the brakes, pulling over to the side. A car honked as it passed them. He turned in his seat, his arm thrown over the seatback, feeling his adrenaline surge. "You know damn well we're way past that. That sucks, Laura. You know what you mean to me. I love you. I love our kids. This isn't an obligation, and you should know that. I just finished showing you, and you're trying to—"

"I know!" Laura shouted back to him, her head in her hands. She was breathing heavy. "I know you love me. I'm sorry, that was a shitty thing to say. I'm just jealous, okay? She's gorgeous, and you were engaged to her?" Her voice shook, and her eyes were wide, filled with questions, uncertainty, and the insecurity he'd thought was long since gone.

"Ten years," he said.

She turned back to him, appearing so confused. "Ten years what?"

"We were engaged," he said, not wanting to have a discussion about this, about Hailey, with Laura. He was so thankful it was the past and not his future. Hailey was not the kind of woman who would stay home and have his babies and let him be the selfish bastard he was. He wanted a woman for him, to be there in his home, raising his kids, being there every moment he walked in, not traipsing around the world.

"You were engaged to her for ten years. Why?" She actually laughed.

"Why does anyone have an engagement that long? Because they know deep down it's anything but the right thing. Besides, she proved me right. She was screwing my foreman almost the entire time."

Laura's mouth gaped.

"Caught them in bed together. Next thing I know, I've got my shotgun out, chased them naked from the staff accommodations, screaming and carrying on. It was a sight. They left town together. Haven't seen her since." He was still shocked that Caroline had inserted Hailey into this game of hers.

"I want to say I'm sorry, but we wouldn't be together then," she said, grinning, and he couldn't help brushing the back of his fingers over her cheek. She leaned in, and he was so grateful for everything that happened that had put Laura in his path. "What was Hailey talking about with the conditions and the property and you walking away? What does this have to do with our kids?"

That was the last thing he wanted to talk about with Laura. She wouldn't be able to hide her hurt from him if she learned how cruel a person his mother was. "Don't worry about it. It's just more irrelevant crap of Caroline's."

He started the engine of Jed's truck and pulled back onto the highway as Laura grabbed her breasts. "Oh, crap, Andy. Sarah's going to need to nurse. Damn, I leaked."

"Won't be long, and she'll have her mama." He reached across the seat, taking in the sight next to him, his wife holding her breasts, needing to feed his baby girl, his T-shirt wet and her damp hair slicked back. Laura was the most beautiful sight he'd ever seen.

ANDY WAS RIGHT. It didn't take long, and as they drove, he reached out to touch her face, her hand. The love from his touch made her feel more sure about their family. She was exhausted from the wave of emotions she'd been drowning in since being back here, though. It seemed to be a feeling of oppression that she'd walked right back into, but this time she felt stronger and more capable, something she'd struggled to get to feel all her life. Was it being with a man like Andy that had allowed her to grow into someone confident, knowing her husband was her shelter from the storm?

The lights were blazing at Jed's as Andy parked beside her minivan and another pickup, a Mercedes, and Diana's SUV. Andy grabbed his bag and reached for Laura's hand before they walked across the darkened yard and into the house, which was alive and filled with life.

"Hey, wondering when you two would get here," Diana said. "Laura, as much as I'd love to hold her forever and she's just precious, she started fussing a few minutes ago, and I'm sorry, my breasts aren't going to work no matter how much I want them to!" She passed a fussing Sarah, who was shoving her fist in her mouth, to Laura. Sarah immediately slipped sideways, pushing at Laura's shirt to nurse.

"Sit down, Laura, in the rocker," Becky said as she appeared from the kitchen, Jeremy hopping beside her, squealing and all smiles when he saw Andy.

"Daddy," he cried, wearing just a shirt and underwear as he raced to Andy, who grabbed him and tossed him in the air and over his shoulder, just as Brad was swinging Chelsea.

"Okay, close quarters tonight, but Mom has been rearranging everyone so they have a spot to sleep," Brad said. He had shed his suit jacket and tie, his white dress shirt rolled up at the sleeves. He was such a handsome man.

Laura pulled up her shirt, letting Sarah latch on. Normally, she was nervous nursing around people, but there was something about this family and the closeness that made her not feel self-conscious. She felt safe and welcome, as if this was where she belonged.

Becky lifted a thin pale baby blanket from a chair back and walked back over to Laura, shaking it out and pressing it over her shoulder the way a mother would. Laura knew Andy wished that Rodney and Becky were his parents, and she too had silently wished the same thing.

"Heard you drove all the way out here with those young ones. Rodney was worried," Becky said as Rodney sat on the sofa across from Laura. "Can't say I wasn't, either."

"I'm sure Andy's glad you're here, but that was a long way for you to drive with young ones alone," Rodney said. "You should have called us, told us you were coming. One of us would have met you."

"Yeah, don't do that again, Laura," Neil said. "As much as I like to tease Andy here and see him come undone, I've never quite seen him…"

"Speechless," Brad said.

"Well, he used a lot of bad words," Diana said as she strode in past Andy, wearing pink sweatpants and a long-sleeved matching shirt. She paused beside Andy and touched his arm. "Seen the same reaction from Jed. You too, Neil and Brad."

"Apparently it's a guy thing." Laura just couldn't help herself as she felt her cheeks pinken, remembering how Andy had made his point. She squeezed her legs together, still feeling the effects of having her husband inside her.

The guys all mumbled something, and Brad winked at her. She should have been mortified, as Diana and Becky laughed. Of course everyone knew what had held them up. Becky sat down beside Rodney, linking her fingers with his hand when he slid his arm around her.

"Andy, Diana wanted to talk with you about all those conditions," Jed said. "She's been reading it all over while waiting for you to show up here." He paused in the hall-way, hands on Gabriel's shoulders, as Danny and Christopher jumped into the room and all the excitement. They had gotten so big. Christopher was the same age as the twins but taller. Danny was two years older. "Time to get these guys to bed," Jed said as Diana leaned down, holding Christopher's arm, saying something to the little boy, who looked like Jed more and more every day.

"Come here." Andy gestured to Gabriel, holding out his other arm for him, and Gabriel walked over, his arms going around Andy's waist. Laura watched her husband, who loved the boy so much it tugged at her heart. "Thanks for helping your mom out. That was a long way to drive."

"I missed you, Dad."

The way Andy was holding Jeremy in one arm and Gabriel against him, she had to swallow the lump jammed in her throat. As much as she loved her husband, there was something so deep about his love for his children, all of them, that was beyond anything she'd ever experienced.

"We should probably do this later and get the kids to bed," Neil said to Brad, sliding his arm around Diana. "Nice to have our very own lawyer for our own personal use, too." He ruffled Diana's hair, which was hanging loosely down her back.

Why did Laura have a feeling that what was coming next was the men sending her off to bed with the kids?

"Neil, go help your brother get the kids to bed," Becky said from where she sat beside Rodney. "Laura, you and Andy are taking Danny's bedroom. Neil and Jed set the crib up for the baby, and there's a double bed in there." It was the new bedroom beside the family room, adding much-needed space to Jed and Diana's cramped house. "The twins are bunking in the family room with their uncle Neil and Danny and Christopher."

"This must be my penance, Mom," Neil said, taking Chelsea from Brad.

"No, it's just you doing your part for the family, Neil, but I know how much you miss your two kids. Brad's taking Christopher's room," Becky added. "Gabriel is coming to stay in the suite above the barn with us tonight."

"So why does Brad get a room to himself and I get

trouble?" Neil teased as he lifted Chelsea in the air, and she giggled.

"Because I'm older and wiser. Not sure it's the better deal, though, getting stuck in a kid's bed," Brad added, standing behind his mom, reaching down and touching her shoulder. She was bright eyed and looking better than she'd looked in Cancun, when they'd gone down for the anniversary. Laura realized she wasn't using a cane anymore.

Sarah had finished nursing on the one breast, and Laura turned her so she could drink from the other.

"Brad, we wouldn't stick you in a toddler bed. You'd break it," Diana said, and everyone laughed. "Jed bought new beds for everyone and stuck double beds in the boys' room so when family came around, you'd have a place to sleep."

"See? The short end of the stick. Jed, you need to add another room," Neil said, and Laura couldn't help smiling, taking in the banter. It was the laughter, the joy, and the closeness of this family that always made her feel that everything bad that happened in the world couldn't exist when they were all together.

Andy put Jeremy down, but Gabriel was still beside him, holding his hand now. "You look tired, bud," Andy said. He was quiet, too. She listened to Andy talk to him, asking him if he had eaten, how he was feeling, resting his hand on his forehead. It was that double checking they always did, worrying that his cancer would come back. "Laura," Andy said, "I'm going to help Jed get the kids to bed. You turn in with Sarah when you're done. I know you're tired."

She was tired, but she was a lot of other things, too. "I am tired. So are you. But when you talk tonight about these conditions, which I can only presume are the same ones Hailey was alluding to, I'll be there." She was proud of herself for how strong her voice sounded.

This was the first time no one said anything, and she noticed the way all the men glanced at each other as if she'd just changed the script. Andy tensed and glanced down at her with a look that was frosty, as if he were about to argue with her, but she wasn't going to back down as she held his gaze.

"Laura…" he started, and she just raised her eyebrows as if daring him to tell her again. He stopped and sighed.

"You're absolutely right, Laura. You should be here," Diana said.

"And I don't need to be," Becky added as she scooted forward. "I'm going to take Gabriel, and we're going to turn in."

"I'll walk you two over there." Rodney helped Becky up and then held out his hand for Gabriel. "Come on, Gabriel. Let's get you settled into bed."

Laura watched as Rodney and Becky slipped on shoes and walked out the front door, heading to the barn, to the suite in the loft that Jed had built. They were the closest thing to grandparents Gabriel had.

"I still don't want you mixed up in this." Andy was leaning down to Laura, his voice low. He was still trying to persuade her, and she couldn't resist reaching up, touching his cheek, taking in the emotion he held in check in his light blue eyes.

"I know you don't, but not knowing is worse, letting my imagination wonder what you're trying to protect me from. She can only hurt us if you let her," she added as he stood up, shaking his head, knowing this wasn't a fight he was going to win.

This time, before he walked away and the twins wrapped their arms around his legs, she realized he didn't seem to hold the same certainty she did. She glanced over at Diana, who was perched on the stool now in front of her.

"I'm right, aren't I?" she asked.

Instead of answering, Diana glanced up at Andy, and no one said a word.

Chapter Twenty

The kids were in bed. The last of the giggles and chatter had died down. Coffee was brewing in the kitchen, and even though Andy would have preferred something stronger, he poured a cup for himself. Laura was in the living room with Diana, sipping a mug of herbal tea. Diana was glowing as she rocked Sarah in her arms.

"You're messing with Diana," Jed said, patting Andy's shoulder as he reached for the pot of coffee and poured a mug for himself, then opened the carton of milk, dumped in a splash, and stirred with a spoon. Jed was becoming more civilized, since at once time he would have just used his finger.

"Excuse me?" He wondered what the hell he'd done now. He had nothing but respect for Diana, a line he'd never cross again.

"Your baby daughter." He jabbed his finger toward Diana, who was smiling down at the baby she was rocking. "She wants one now."

Andy smiled and took a sip from his coffee, feeling

relieved it wasn't something else. "I'm sure that's something you can take care of." He nudged Jed.

"She wants a daughter. She loves the boys, but she really wants a girl. She went on and on about it when we brought the baby back here. She wouldn't even let Mom hold her."

Andy couldn't help being proud. He couldn't help feeling as if he had everything. "She is pretty special."

"Diana's claimed Sarah again?" Neil appeared and opened the fridge door, pulling out a beer. He twisted the cap off and tossed it in the trash. "I expect next time to hear that Diana will be expecting again."

The corner of Jed's lips quirked in amusement, as he took another swallow of coffee, watching his wife cuddle the baby sleeping soundly in her arms.

Brad appeared in the front room next just as the door closed and Rodney strode in. Both noticed Diana enraptured and smiled. "Nothing better than a houseful of kids, a sleeping quiet baby. Doesn't get any better," Rodney said. Then he was in the kitchen with Brad, and they were laughing about something.

Diana glanced over to Jed, and Jed nodded to her as if they each knew what the other was thinking. "As much as I want to hold her all night, I suppose you should put her to bed," she said, slipping the sleeping baby to Laura, who stepped out of the room to put the baby down.

The living room was cozy and small, and Andy took a spot on the loveseat by the window. Diana left the room as Brad and Neil took up a spot on each end of the sofa. Rodney took the rocker, which creaked from his weight. "Careful there, Dad," Brad teased.

"Mom didn't want to stay for this? She didn't come for the funeral, either. What's up with that?" Neil asked, and

Rodney just shook his head. "She came for the kids, her grandkids. It's where she'd rather be."

For a minute, by the way he said it and the odd expression on Rodney's face, Andy wondered if there was more. Maybe she wasn't feeling well. "You sure you're okay with Gabriel?" Andy asked.

"He's a great kid, Andy. Becky was reading him a story when I left. They're having a great time." He smiled. "We should really get to the heart of the matter. Andy, the family your mother comes from wields a lot of power. It's an empire that's being passed to you."

"It's being given with conditions that are outrageous," Diana said as she walked back in, wearing glasses, holding the documents, the will and conditions that had been provided to Andy. She stood in front of Jed, who slipped his arms around her, leaning his chin on the top of her head. They swayed together, and he looked down at the documents as she flipped the page, pointing out something.

"Basically, what this is all about, Andy, is your mother once again trying to run your life and arrange it how it best suits her," Diana said. "I've gone through the will, the conditions. She had a team of lawyers draft this up, and as ludicrous as this sounds, it's legally binding. The question comes down to a choice, really, of you deciding whether you want the next two years of your life to be dictated to you, because it's clear in all the fine print that you must reside at the estate here full time. There's no loophole for living somewhere else, and the number of days and nights you're to remain are clear, as is who can't live there with you…"

"You mean me." Laura walked in and looked to Diana before glancing over at Andy.

"Diana," he said, wanting her to stop and not say another word when the flash of hurt flickered over Laura's expression. He slid forward, resting his elbows on his knees. "Laura, it doesn't matter what she wants to happen. It's not even an issue." He held out his hand, and Laura hesitated only a second before crossing to him, sitting down beside him. He reached for her hand when she went to clasp them together.

"I'd like to know what all the conditions are." She actually held up her hand to Diana, who appeared surprised.

"I don't know if that's a good idea, Laura. I felt sick reading them and couldn't imagine what I'd do if this were me in your spot."

"It's not going to happen anyway, Laura. You think I would even consider money, power, everything over my family?" he said, but she had a stubbornness on her face as she insisted on seeing the conditions.

Diana looked to Andy as if she wanted him to do something, and then she handed the conditions to Laura. He watched as she read through the list, her face flushing. Neil and Brad were shaking their heads.

"So that was why Hailey was insistent on meeting with you. Your mother is doing her best even from the grave to get rid of me. Put a woman in your path you had a past with, hoping the spark would still be there and you'd stray." She handed the papers back to Diana, who lifted her glasses on top of her head.

"We don't stray, Laura," Brad said from where he sat on the sofa, his arm tossed over the back as he looked to Andy, Jed, and then Neil as if speaking for all of them.

"So you're willing to give up everything for me, for Gabriel?" She swallowed, and he wondered how long it would take him to convince her that it wasn't even a choice.

"Seriously, Laura, how can you even think I would consider those conditions? Living apart from you, from

Gabriel, who is my son, because some sick, twisted woman is still trying to control me?" He said it a little too loudly, and Jed gave him a warning glance. The kids, of course.

Laura appeared so sad when she looked to him. "So what happens to everything if you say no?"

"I've already said no. It doesn't matter," he said, because thinking about people losing their jobs was the only thing that had bothered him and made him wonder for a second whether there was another way.

"You didn't answer me," she said, and he couldn't help wondering why she'd care what happened to all the vast wealth Caroline was dangling in front of them.

"You're worried about the money?"

"I'm not interested in all that, Andy, but are you sure you wouldn't one day be angry with me because you tossed it all away?"

He had to look over to Neil, who had done some things that were twisted and sick, but he'd done everything out of love. He was the cousin he related to out of all of them, the one so much like him at times they could have been brothers. "How could I be? Family is everything."

Neil nodded in agreement.

"I don't think you understand, Laura. Stuff is just stuff, but you and the kids are family. The estate, everything she owns will be liquidated, sold off, and passed on to her brothers." He glanced over to Rodney. "And Todd is going to have to figure out how to stand on his own two feet."

"He'll be just fine, Andy. My brother and I may come from the same mother, but we are as different as two human beings can be."

"Great. That's the way I like business to be, simple and to the point," Neil added, maybe to break the tension in the room. "Diana, don't forget to bill this bum for your time, and make sure you charge for all incidentals: dinner, food, drinks…"

She rolled her eyes, clutching the papers. "As if I'm going to charge family. Andy, I'll let the lawyers know your answer tomorrow."

He didn't say anything for a minute as he reached for Laura's hand again. "You know what, Diana? I have a few things to take care of tomorrow, so if you don't mind, I'll tell them." He squeezed Laura's hand and patted it as she frowned. "Sometimes when you close a door, you have to slam it shut."

When he glanced up across the room to Neil, who was watching him with a shrewdness he recognized and welcomed, there was also understanding. "Then we're going home," he said, "where we belong."

Chapter Twenty-One

"You sure you want to do this?" Neil asked as he closed the door of Diana's SUV, into which Brad, Rodney, Jed, and Andy had piled to drive back to the estate to meet the lawyers just after breakfast.

Rodney was the first up the stone steps to the door, which opened before he could knock.

"Glad you called and said you were coming," Todd said. He was standing there, holding the door open. "Brad, Jed, Neil, didn't have much of a chance to talk yesterday."

"Uncle Todd," Brad said, then turned to Andy, who stopped just outside the door. "Coming?"

"You know what? I'll be right in," Andy said. He needed a minute. Maybe Brad understood his hesitation, as he nodded and somehow directed Todd into the house. Neil stayed with him outside. Andy let out a sigh, looking up at the estate and then over to Neil, who had given everything he owned, almost, to the surrogate who'd carried his son, Michael. He wondered then how Neil could have just given it away, walked away from a fortune he'd created. He understood now.

"This was such a nice place, all stone and massive and cold. Not easy to walk away from it," Neil said. "Tell me, didn't you have even a moment where you considered how you could have everything?"

Coming from anyone else, he'd have been furious, but Neil was different.

"I grew up knowing this would be mine. Living with this and, sure, having that kind of fortune behind you can go to your head. Maybe there was a nanosecond of thinking what I could leave my kids and give Laura." Then he pictured his mother and the iciness he'd grown up with. She'd never once held him, hugged him, or shown him any genuine affection. She'd broken his heart as a child raised by servants.

"That's all?" Neil sounded disgusted.

"I've already given my children the greatest gift."

Neil appeared confused for a minute.

"Their mother," Andy said.

Neil smiled and rested his hand on Andy's shoulder. "That you have. Shall we get this over with?"

Andy walked with Neil into the mansion, taking a look at everything, the artwork, the furnishings, the glitter that went with a place like this.

"In here," Jed called from the doorway of the library, appearing as if he were ready to leave now.

The maid was there, serving coffee. Hailey was smiling and chatting with Brad. She looked classy in her dress pants, a deep pink ruffled tank top, and her blond hair piled high in a chignon. She had huge gold hoops and the same brilliant smile he remembered.

Blair was chatting with Rodney, and two other men were there who introduced themselves as the managing partners from his mother's law firm.

"Glad you're all here," Andy said. "I won't take much

of your time. Thought it would be better in person. Those conditions outlined by Caroline are completely unacceptable."

Todd swore under his breath, and Hailey gasped.

"Andy, you haven't really thought this through clearly," the dark-haired senior partner said.

"Well, that's where you're wrong. It's not even a question of thinking it through. I have a wife, children, and a family I love. This is just stuff and means nothing. You really think I would trade in my life, as good as it is, as happy as I am, with a woman I love, who loves me, for this? For the life of misery my mother chose?" He shook his head, sad at the waste.

"Andy, you never tried," Todd said. "This kind of birthright doesn't happen to the average person. Very few people come into the kind of wealth and power you have. You think I wanted this kind of life? I made it work for you because of what you were going to have." He couldn't believe his father had said that. "Rodney, talk some sense into the boy. There are a lot of secrets that are best kept where they are. You know this. You agreed."

Andy was looking from his uncle to his father, wondering what was going on between them. Even Brad and Neil appeared confused. He found himself walking over to Jed, who didn't seem too happy. "What's this about?" he asked, but Jed was shaking his head.

"No idea. Not sure I want to know."

"It's Andy's choice, Todd," Rodney said. "You made your bed a long time ago. You decided who you wanted to be."

Todd was leaning against the mantle, running his hand through his hair. "There never was a choice with old Angus. You know that."

Even Brad frowned over at Neil. No one seemed to

have any idea what was going on or what their grandfather had to do with this. Angus Friessen had been a Washington state senator and a rancher, raising two sons.

"You were the one who was left everything," Todd said. "I can't help thinking if the tables were turned, it would be me with your life, all of it…"

This was the first time Andy had seen Rodney this angry. Brad must have known, as he stopped his dad with his hand to his chest before he made it halfway across the room.

"Whoa, Dad, what the hell?" Brad shouted, and Neil was there, too, holding him back, both looking from Rodney to Todd. There was something in the air between them and something else in the words Todd was saying. Andy knew there was way more going on. He had grown up with Todd, knowing his ways.

"You may have married her, but I loved her," Todd said.

What the fuck?

He wasn't sure who yelled or who threw the punch, but Todd was on the floor, and Brad and Neil had a hold of Rodney, whom they were pulling back and yelling at. The table had been kicked over, and Jed was yelling, too. The two lawyers were helping Todd up. Blair had Hailey back in the corner.

"We're leaving now!" Andy said, grabbing Jed's shoulder and shaking him, feeling how tightly wound he was. What the hell was his dad doing? He couldn't believe he'd just said he loved Becky, Rodney's wife. This was an all-time low, even for his father.

"Andy, we're leaving!" Neil shouted from the door. He turned to where Jed was halfway to the door, and he could see Brad outside, already talking with Rodney, maybe trying to find out what claim Todd thought he had on their mother.

"Give me a second." Andy said, turning back to his father and to Blair, who was standing with Hailey and the two lawyers, who were talking to Todd as he dabbed at the blood dripping from his mouth. He wondered who had punched him, Jed, Rodney, or Brad. It had happened so fast.

"Would you all excuse us for a minute?" he said. He didn't have to ask a second time, as everyone left him alone in the library with his father. His mind blanked. "Why would you do that to your brother?" He was shaking his head. "And what was that about my aunt?" He gestured to the door.

"Your uncle, the oldest son, never had to work for much. He was given the ranch, the money. And he got the girl."

He just stared at his father, waiting for him to say what he feared he would. "Did you sleep with her too?" *Please say no.*

"He ignored her. He didn't know the good thing he had with her. I fell in love with her, but she wouldn't leave him."

He shut his eyes, feeling the illusion of the image he had of Rodney and Becky and their idealistic life together shatter. *Please, no.*

"She was a good woman. Is a good woman. And my brother, who had everything, was more interested in stoking her jealousy. Paid more attention to a neighbor woman. He was selfish…"

"And you moved in," he said, because he knew well how Todd operated with women. He'd seen him, the interest, saying all the right things, setting some woman up in a house somewhere, one mistress after the other, but never once had he said he loved any of them.

"I was visiting. I listened to her and watched as my brother ignored her."

He didn't know what to say as a horn honked from outside, but he also didn't want to stay in here and listen to any more about a woman he respected and now couldn't help feeling disappointed in. How could he look at her now without feeling disgust? He started toward the door.

"She wasn't like the rest, Andy. She was special. For the first time in my life, I walked away, and then I met your mother."

He turned back in the archway, gesturing wildly with his hands. "And what, you want me to pat you on the back and say good for you? Seriously, Dad." He just shook his head. "I've got to go." He looked across the room to his father, who looked so much like his uncle. His father, a man he'd been close with at one time. Such a waste.

"You love her?" his father asked him as he walked around the sofa, closer to Andy, his lip beginning to swell. "Laura."

"Yeah, more than you could ever understand."

"You'd walk away from all this for her?" His dad wasn't pleading or shouting.

"You can't buy love. You should know that," he said, and he turned without another word and pulled open the front door.

"Andy," his father called out again, his footsteps echoing on the tile. "I hope she's worth it." He put his hands on his hips. "Stay in touch?"

Andy just looked at his father and walked out the door.

Chapter Twenty-Two

The sweeping views from the back deck that Jed had built went down into a large fenced-off yard that was all grass, with a tire swing hanging from a sturdy branch on the oak tree. All the kids were running around in the sunshine and the warm fall air, barefoot, with grass-stained pants and rosy cheeks from the fun they were having.

Diana was carrying Sarah in her arm as she set a pitcher of tea on the patio table. "Becky is resting inside. She fell asleep in the rocker. I think the kids wore her out."

"Is she okay?" Laura couldn't help worrying about Andy's aunt, who'd suffered a stroke shortly after Laura first found out she was pregnant with Sarah. It had been hard on Andy, all of the family, as they gathered to her bedside. She had been a miracle.

"Yeah, she's just trying to live every day, she said, as if there's no tomorrow. She said that was one of the good things that came out of lying in a hospital bed with one foot on the other side. She appreciates the little things. She visits her grandkids often. It's nice having her and Rodney here."

Sarah was cooing and then giggled when Diana kissed her tummy and then pretended to put her tiny foot in her mouth and bite her toes.

"I can take her, you know," Laura said, but she was enjoying being here with Diana, watching the kids play, just being with a family that meant everything to her.

"Not a chance. You and Andy are going to leave soon, and when am I going to get to see her again? I'm so jealous of you having a daughter. I just never realized how much I wanted my own." She glanced up and across the yard. "Christopher, not so high!" she called out as her youngest climbed the tree. The twins were on the tire swing, and Danny was pushing as Gabriel followed Christopher up and over the branches.

"You worry they're going to fall."

Diana gave her a disgusted look. "All the time! The first time I looked out the window and Danny was up in the top of the tree, I was screaming and Jed came running. I'm thinking one wrong step, and he falls and he's dead, but Jed calmly goes over and tells him to keep his foot on the branch close to the trunk where it's strong and climb down, then asks him if he knows what a widow maker is."

Laura realized then that she was glad they didn't have any trees close to the house.

"Then the rule was enforced that they can't climb higher than the roofline. Still, my heart beats a little faster every time they climb it. But, Jed reminds me, they're boys, and this is what boys do. I wonder how Becky did it and managed to stay sane, raising three of them."

Laura smiled, listening to Diana and the way she was enamored with her daughter.

"I want another baby, a daughter, but there are no guarantees," she said, smiling brightly at Laura.

"You'd be disappointed with a boy?"

"Are you kidding? I wouldn't trade them for anything, but I still want a daughter. I don't know, maybe to experience that mother–daughter relationship that you only hear about. I never had that, and I want a daughter to share things with."

"You never had it easy," Laura said to Diana, who only smiled and shrugged.

"No, but I got past it. I have a great life. She just kind of sent me in a tailspin, showing up at my door, pretending to care, still being the same selfish woman she's always been. It hurt to think I could be like her, however messed up that sounds."

"You're a beautiful woman, Diana, and you were the first one who reached out to me and tried to help me. I'll never forget that. Don't ever doubt who you are. You're my inspiration."

She'd never seen Diana so humbled. "Wow, I'm speechless. Thank you." Diana cleared her throat. "Now if I can just remember your words of wisdom the next time my mother shows up here…"

The sound of a vehicle driving in had Diana turning her head, her face tensing.

"When I saw you in Cancun for the anniversary and you said your mother had showed up at your door… Diana, I've never seen you so upset," Laura said. "And to hear what you went through as a child, your loss, I guess I just understood that Jed was going to make sure she didn't bother you again."

Diana got up just as she heard the men's voices and footsteps. Then there was relief on her face.

"Has she been back?" Laura asked, realizing something else was worrying Diana.

She nodded. "It's just something I have to take care of."

She didn't get a chance to question Diana more when Jed appeared, and this time Diana handed Sarah back to her. Whatever was bothering Diana, she wanted her to finally have the peace she deserved.

"Let's get lunch started. Who wants a burger?" Neil called out as he went over to the barbecue and fired it up. When he turned back to Laura, he winked in that outrageously flirty way of his. "You're good for Andy" was all he said before he called the kids and left her alone with her thoughts.

Chapter Twenty-Three

The fire crackled as the crickets sang in chorus. It was dark, and the stars were bright. He stared at the house, the lights blazing where the kids were asleep. He took another breath of the night, sitting around the fire with his thoughts as he tried to make sense of the day.

He watched Jed in the window as he slipped his arms around Diana, kissed her, and then started out the back door.

"You heading out at first light?" Brad had been quiet for so long, sitting around the fire with Neil, whittling a stick. Rodney was leaning back in his chair, staring up at the stars.

"Bright and early. Shove the kids in their seats while they're still asleep. Hopefully we'll make it back before dark," Andy said.

Everyone had been quiet, and no one had said a word although he knew every one of them was trying to make sense of what they had learned about Becky and Todd. It was something he wished he'd never come to know, the legacy his father had selfishly shared.

"You?" Jed said. There was nothing left in his beer, and Jed had two in his hand when he joined them again. "Anyone?" he asked, holding the extra out.

Andy just shook his head. He was done, not really feeling it tonight. Brad shook his head, but Neil reached out and took the beer, clinking the bottle with Jed and saying, "Thank you, brother."

"We'll leave in the morning, probably not long after you," Brad said. "Got to get back. Em's holding down the fort. You talk to Candy?" He turned to Neil.

"Yeah, she was having dinner with Em. Guess Emily was trying to talk her into staying over, a girls' night."

He couldn't help smiling, thinking of living close to family again. Would be nice.

Jed was standing, staring down at the fire, glancing over to Rodney, who had been quiet all night. Brad widened his eyes, and Neil rubbed his face as if someone needed to say something, but no one had a clue what to say.

"Suppose you're wanting some answers," Rodney said.

Jed tossed a piece of wood on the fire and kicked at the coals with his worn cowboy boot. "Kind of, Dad."

"You're probably thinking some awful things." Rodney was still looking up at the sky, his hands behind his head, leaning back in the bright orange Adirondack chair.

"Don't know what to think, Dad." Neil was resting his elbows on his knees, dangling the beer in his hand, shaking his head.

"Your grandfather was a mean son of a bitch," Rodney said as if he were speaking to the sky. "He had plans and everything laid out. The ranch you have now, Brad, was his decree. Passed on to the oldest son." He was shaking his head. "Angus was not a warm man with a lot of feelings. He was a senator, the president of the cattlemen's association, and he had big boots to fill."

No one said anything, but they were looking at one another as if waiting for Rodney to continue.

"It's always been done the same way in families. Goes back to the beginning of time. The firstborn son shall inherit the earth, and God forbid if you're a girl." He sat up and rested his hands on the arms of the chair, looking into the fire. "Never would have considered another way. But the way your grandfather decreed his will, there was no choice for you boys." He looked to Jed and Neil. "Your grandfather decided it would go to the firstborn son. Even the deed you have, Brad, doesn't allow for a girl to have the property. Never really thought much about it until this mess with your mother, Andy."

He should say something, but instead he just rested in the chair, staring into the fire.

"Your mother…" Rodney started and then stopped, as if he couldn't get the words out, and this time Brad was staring at his dad with both fury and worry, an emotion Andy was all too familiar with.

"I didn't treat your mother very well. Apparently I took after my dad in ways I'm not proud of. I was full of myself, arrogant, cocky, married to a catch who was gorgeous, and she stole my heart. I dumped her at the ranch and just expected her to be happy, and I did whatever the hell I pleased. There was a neighbor woman always calling for help, and your mother was jealous, and I shouldn't have gone, but there was something about being needed that way by a pretty woman and then going home to another."

"Dad, if you tell me you cheated on Mom…" Neil wouldn't look at his dad, but Andy could tell how bothered he was.

"No, I never crossed that line. Doesn't mean I didn't want to, because me and your mother were about as far apart then as any two can get. I hated going home to her accusations, and the fighting. Being with that neighbor woman made me feel as if I was wanted again, but sleeping with a woman when married to another is…" This time, his uncle looked at each one of them as if he was trying to make them understand. "There are just some lines you don't cross. At least I was smart enough to know that, but that didn't stop me from letting your mother think I was cheating, which is just as bad. Every one of us has something we've done in our past we wish we could go back and undo. Your mother and I were young and foolish in a lot of ways."

"So you didn't cheat. Did Mom?" Neil wasn't going to leave it alone.

Rodney scrunched his eyes, and a tear rolled down his cheek. Andy had never seen his uncle cry, and he watched the horror on Brad's face as he sat across from his father.

"My brother showed up, young and dashing, and he gave her an ear. He listened to her." Rodney gestured at the fire. "He was doing what I should have been doing. My mistake was letting him stay, and maybe I knew and I didn't care at the time, because we were drifting apart. I thought I had it all, looking down on a brother who had nothing and had to make his own way. Yes, they had an affair under my roof, right under my nose."

Andy shut his eyes, feeling ill, thinking of the aunt he loved and the crumbling pedestal she was on.

"He left one day, and then everything just kind of exploded. It was tense, and I knew there was something, because she had been watching my brother the way she used to look at me. It was weeks that passed, and she'd lock herself in the bathroom and cry for hours." He shut his eyes, shoving his hands through his white hair, which was now sticking up. "Your mother never wanted you to know any of this. Neither did I. This was a secret of ours, our past. Something we're not proud of."

"Sounds to me like there's more, Dad." Jed had been pretty quiet as he stared into the fire.

"She was pregnant," Rodney said.

Jed made a strangled sound. Neil choked on his beer.

"It wasn't any of you."

Andy was staring at his uncle, knowing if his dad had had any idea, there may have been an entirely different outcome.

"I lost it. Damn near beat her. She was cowering and screaming. So were you two." Rodney looked over to Brad and Neil.

Andy couldn't help watching Jed a little closer.

"I grabbed my shotgun with every intention of hunting down my brother and shooting him. I planned on dumping his body and burying it where it would never be found, but your mother may have saved us both." Rodney took a breath. "She called the sheriff, who caught up with me and tossed me in a cell overnight to cool off. He let me out in the morning, kept my shotgun and sent me home. When I walked in, I believed it was over, and there was your mother, standing in the living room, calm. You kids were there, settled, and I stepped in and just stared at her for I don't know how long before I noticed the blood dripping from her arms."

No one was watching the fire, because every one of them was glued to what Rodney was saying.

"If I'd been another hour, she'd have been dead."

"Dad, I...I don't know what to say," Brad said, and he sounded as confused as Andy was.

"She spent a week locked up in a psych ward. She lost the baby, and it was a turning point for us. Her parents came out, and it was her daddy who sat me down after learning all the ugly truth and all the bullshit I'd added to it. He made me figure out what it was about her that I loved, or else that was it. He was ending our marriage, taking you, Brad and Neil, back to California. I realized then that I loved her, and I sat there at a table with her father, a reasonable man, a man who was a far better husband and father than I had been. I wanted to do better. We made it work, your mother made it work. We found our way back to each other, but we built something stronger, something solid and real. Then we had you, Jed."

Rodney looked up at them. "So please don't ever think less of your mother. It would kill her to know you know. We've shared this only once." Rodney stopped and glanced over to Neil. "With Candy."

Brad rustled in his chair, and Neil turned to his father for the first time, appearing speechless.

"My wife knows, and she didn't tell me?"

"Your wife knows because she was going to leave you, and I needed to be the man your mother's father was. He was a good man. Your mother is so proud of each one of you." His gaze even landed on Andy. "Especially you, Andy. Watching you with that young woman you chose, we're proud."

Neil appeared shell shocked, sitting across the fire. "Why didn't she tell me?"

"You nearly destroyed all that goodness with Candy because of your obsession. It was like looking in a mirror of who I used to be. Be smarter. Learn from my mistakes, from your own, and don't make them again." He pushed out of the chair and stretched. "I trust this will stay between us."

Jed reached over and squeezed his dad's shoulder but didn't say a word.

"Then I'll say goodnight," Rodney said. "It's been a long day, and I think I'll turn in."

"Goodnight, Dad," Brad said as his father walked away. Then he reached out with his foot, kicking Neil's booted one. "Cut it out."

"I can't believe Candy didn't say anything." Neil appeared betrayed.

"You heard Dad. That's not the kind of thing you go and share. 'Hey, dear, guess what? Your mom had an affair and tried to kill herself.' Seriously, Neil, I'm trying to figure out how to understand this. What to say to Mom, what not to say," Brad said, shaking his head.

"How about nothing?" Andy said, sitting there, taking it all in. Hearing it now, he started to piece together some things, a sadness he'd always wondered about with his aunt, with Rodney. "Hearing only part of it today, I imagined the worst, but it's more." He gestured at his cousins. "Every one of us has fucked something up big time and done something we wish we could bury so everyone forgets. Your parents are everything mine aren't. A good man is someone who's flawed and who's made mistakes but has enough courage to make it right and try his damnedest to never do it again. Your mom and dad are an example of commitment and love and understanding. I mean, how can you really understand unless you've done those same awful things?" Andy pushed out of his chair and took in the shocked expressions on his three cousins' faces. If they only knew all the secrets—and his mother's, too, the life she had chosen to hide.

"You surprise the hell out of me sometimes, Andy," Brad said. "What are you going to do?"

"I'm going to bed, and then in the morning, I'm taking my family home," he said, and he walked away, breathing in the night air, feeling as if the burden of the past and the secrets he had held on to had lifted.

He had the love of a good wife, a houseful of children. He really was a wealthy man.

Chapter 24

COMING HOME

"Where the hell did all this water come from?" Andy said as he took another step into the kitchen, looking at the puddle on the floor and the water splattered over the counter and stove, none of which had any business being there.

"Daddy, what's this?" Jeremy tried to run past him and skidded through the puddle.

"Whoa there, bud!" Andy lifted him in his arms before he could have the fun only a toddler just a few months shy of his third birthday could have. He tried to imagine how his innocent little boy viewed this as fun and exciting rather than a mess, a potential disaster of their house falling apart. "What the…" He was still holding Jeremy as he looked at the mess, at the water dripping from his ceiling. "Oh no."

"Andy, what is it?" Laura said, coming in behind him, carrying the baby.

"Keep everyone out. We got a problem, a water leak or something." He put Jeremy down and tapped his little butt.

"Go on and play with your sister in the living room. Stay out of here for now."

Andy could hear Laura directing the kids. Gabriel was in another room, and the twins were chattering away, more interested in seeing what disaster had befallen their house than in playing. After some tearful goodbyes and a full day of driving home from Jed's, still haunted by what he'd learned about his beloved aunt and his father, Andy wanted nothing more than to relax, have some dinner, and unwind with his wife after the kids were asleep. It looked like none of that was about to happen now.

"Oh no, where's it coming from?" Laura was back, touching Andy's arm as he stepped around the center island in the kitchen, looking at the droplets and the stain now spreading across the ceiling.

"Could be a burst pipe," he said—or maybe the entire ceiling was about to come down. "Do you see any leaks anywhere else?" He looked around the kitchen, the dining room, and the family room but didn't see anything. Good news, sort of.

"Maybe you should call a plumber?" Laura said as Gabriel started into the kitchen, and she just as quickly turned him around and sent him on his way. "Gabriel, no. Let your dad see what's going on. Did you take your bag to your room?"

"On my bed, Mom. Are we having dinner?" he asked. The kids had to be hungry after driving all day, only stopping for snacks twice. Andy had driven the last three hours home without pause.

"Okay, no one is going into the kitchen, though," Andy said. "I'm going to call a plumber, and we'll go into town for supper."

"Andy, I don't think we're going to get the kids back in their car seats. I know I've had about enough. Why don't we just barbecue some burgers outside? Then we're not in the kitchen, and the kids can run around and burn off all this restlessness."

Smart woman he'd married. Of course, she was right. The kids would be unsettled and fussy. Barbecue would be great. He could let the plumber deal with the problem inside and keep the kids out.

He took a look at his smart, sexy wife, glad she was with him, had chosen him, and loved him. She had given him the second chance he hadn't deserved. She smiled right back at him before he heard a hiss, and a chunk of drywall fell from the ceiling, crashing onto the center island. He jumped back, taking Laura with him, drenched by a splatter of water the likes of which he'd never seen.

Chapter 25

Coming home after spending time with Andy's family was so welcome—but walking into water damage was far from the ideal situation. Andy had managed to contact a plumber and get him out within the hour, which would cost him, of course. Even though Andy handled all the finances, he never worried about what they spent, and Laura had to catch herself whenever she saw the amounts. The plumber had been efficient, though, having replaced the plastic pipe that had been damaged by a chewing rat, which she was still horrified about. Worse, the rat was still inside the tresses, as she heard Andy and the plumber saying. It could be looking for more pipes to chew on, so they'd need an exterminator and a drywaller to repair the damage.

Not the welcome home she'd imagined.

Andy was in the shower when Laura walked into their bedroom. The kids were fast asleep, worn out after running outside in between bites of their burgers and burning off restless energy from being cooped up most of the day. Sarah was down after her last feeding, hopefully for six hours, at least. Laura wanted nothing more than to strip out of her clothes and climb into bed and go to sleep, but there was something about Andy since they had pulled away from Jed and Diana's that seemed unusually distracted.

She slipped out of her clothes, tossed them in the hamper, and pushed open the bathroom door, seeing Andy through the shower glass, his arm against the wall, leaning his head down under the spray in a way that let her know he was contemplating something. It was clear to her that something was bothering him.

When she pulled open the glass door, he turned his head out of the water, appearing surprised at first as her hand went to his stomach and chest, touching him and feeling the perfection, the strength, and the brooding that all were, at times, her Andy.

"Kids asleep?" he asked her as he stepped aside, allowing the hot water to spray down on her.

"Mmm." It was so invigorating and relaxing at the same time, being able to wash off the day's grime. "Yeah, fast asleep, all of them." She tilted her head back under the spray, rinsing out her hair, feeling her husband's gaze burn into her. He never hid his interest or tried, for Andy was a man with a sexual appetite that rivalled hers. At times, she was almost embarrassed by how much she needed him.

As she stared back at this man she loved so much and into the heat pouring back to her, she wished Andy would start to open up more and share with her some of the things she knew he held on to, but he wasn't a talker or a sharer, and he always wanted—no, needed to fix everything and anything that came their way.

"Would love to know what's going through your mind," Laura said.

Andy didn't say a word, his expression the same hardness she'd come to understand was his way of hiding what he was thinking. He slipped his hand around her back and pulled her to him so she could feel every hard inch of him that was ready for her. He lowered his head and kissed her, not in a soft, loving way but roughly, deeply, brutally in a way that marked her and made every thought she'd had moments before vanish.

She was lost in feeling when he had her backed against the tiled shower wall, about to lift her. She broke the kiss, breathing hard as Andy pressed in closer, his eyes on her lips, taking in her face, her gaze, holding on to it with such raw hunger. The man was positively primal.

She wasn't ready. She wanted to talk as he lifted her, spreading her wide, and she felt him shift, about to enter her. "Andy, why won't you talk?"

He paused a second before moving inside her, holding himself still as she gripped his shoulders. "The only talking I want to do is this," he said, and he made his point by pulling out and slamming back into her, forcing the breath out of her. It was rough and wild, and she loved it, the times he became like this. These were times when he only wanted to feel, to lose himself in her, and she wondered whether it was so he couldn't feel the hurt or worry or whatever it was he was so deeply enmeshed in. Was this the only way to give him the peace he needed in this moment?

He kissed her neck before tugging on her ear with his teeth, moving inside her again.

Her legs locked around his waist. "Oh, Andy, you feel so good," she said, but he didn't answer as he used her body for his need, to appease himself.

For a moment, she realized the only talking he needed right now was this touch, with her. If she tried to explain his need to anyone, they'd see it as him using her, but then, no one knew Andy as well as she did. He was a difficult man, headstrong, domineering at times, and would do anything for her. That kind of love and devotion in a man was a gift, one those who didn't know Andy could never understand.

As much as she needed him, leaned on him, and depended on him, Andy needed her, too.

Chapter 26

It was still dark, and he didn't need to open his eyes to know Laura was awake behind him, her warm skin and firm breasts nestled against his back. Her hand was now skimming over his arm so softly that it tickled as she pressed a kiss into the back of his shoulder.

"Why are you awake?" he said, surprised. He'd slept all he could, considering how wound up he was, but losing himself in Laura was almost a drug he needed to free his mind from his worries just for a while.

"Wondering if you'll ever tell me what's going on," she whispered.

How could she even begin to understand what she was asking of him? "Nothing for you to worry about," he said. He didn't want to push her away, though he expected her to retreat from him, as she did at times when he wouldn't share what he was thinking. This time, she slid her hand over his stomach, pressing closer to him.

Sighing, she said, "Andy, I won't break, but I also know when you're carrying the weight of something. And I know you'll handle it, so if that's the next thing out of your mouth, I'm way ahead of you."

He had to smile, because it would have been. Maybe she could feel his response, he wasn't sure, but she pressed closer, raising herself up on her elbow, her hair brushing over his arm as she leaned down and kissed his cheek. He didn't expect the tenderness, and that made him feel like crap for using her body the way he needed to, pounding into her over and over. She was his wife, his love, the first place he could go to forget everything. He hoped she'd never know what a bastard he could be because of his need for her.

"Something happened with your family is all I can think of," she said. "You walked away from a lot for me…"

He couldn't listen to this. He rolled on his back and rested his hands on her arms, holding her, looking at her. "I walked away from nothing that was really mine, so stop it about this being for you. We're a family. There isn't a choice when someone is trying to drive a wedge between us. Money can't buy love or happiness—just stuff." It was nothing he wanted, all that privilege and parties, rubbing elbows with the super rich. He wasn't interested, and he pitied his mother for the person she had become, for choosing that world.

"Okay, I get that, but what is it, then, if not the money? Because I can tell with you, the way you are with me. You become all handsy and caveman like when you're struggling or bothered by something, not like I'm complaining. I love the sex with you when you're trying to lose yourself in me."

He couldn't believe what he was hearing, what she was saying as she slid on top of him to lie on him as if he were her bed. Of course his hands went right to her ass, feeling every curve over her rounded bottom. She had the best ass now. After four children, it was plump and round and firm. She had one of the greatest bodies he'd ever seen. "You love it?" he said. "Seriously? Because I worry sometimes after that I'm too rough, and you say nothing."

"Mmm," she said, kissing his chest as he felt himself stirring again from her touch. "Never, you could never hurt me. I love all the ways you are, Andy, never the same, always surprising, always extremely satisfying."

He rolled her over onto her back, and her legs went around his waist as if they knew where they had to be. He could just take her again. She was ready and willing.

Her hand pressed into his chest. "But I still want to know what it is that happened, because there had to have been something more. Knowing your family, I've seen what they're capable of."

He pulled away and lay down on his back, his arm pressed into his forehead. Why was she harping on this? He didn't want this in his head anymore.

"I don't want to upset you," she said, "but you thinking that keeping it from me is going to protect me, well, you're wrong."

"I found out my family isn't as twisted as I thought," he said.

"Ah, okay. What does that mean?" She was touching him again, her foot rubbing his leg.

"It means my parents' entire marriage was a business arrangement of some sort. My father was paid to marry my mom and provide an heir, me." He sighed, not wanting to think anymore about being a product of that union. "And my mother had this deep dark secret her father would have done anything to hide, which is the reason for my father and her marrying. She was into women, not men." His aunt and his father had also had a secret affair, but he couldn't ever tell anyone about that.

Laura lifted his arm from where he had covered his face with it. "Seriously?"

He couldn't see her face or the shocked expression he knew had to be pasted there. "Just preserving the image of the family," he said.

Her touch was so tender as she linked her fingers with his. "Well, I have to say I'm shocked and then horrified for you, but I'm grateful, too."

What could she mean by that?

She squeezed his hand tighter. "Because you wouldn't be here if all that hadn't happened, and I'm so very happy to have met you. I can only imagine your surprise and that you're bothered by it, but I guess having it another way could have meant you wouldn't be here, and what would I do then? I love you and our life."

God, he was so in love with this woman. Did she have any idea, saying what she did, what it meant to him? "You have an odd way of making me look at something in a good light," he said, and he laughed, reaching for her and pulling her onto him.

She leaned forward and kissed him so tenderly. Breaking the kiss, she started to pull away until he reached behind her head, holding her close. "And now you can show me just how much you love me," she said. She squealed as he moved inside her, and this time, he let her set the pace.

Chapter 27

"I'm telling you I have no idea how they're disappearing. I've ridden the entire fence line, and there's no downed sections. It's as if they're just vanishing into thin air."

Laura was washing the frypan left from breakfast, glancing up at the ceiling and the hole left by the plumber the night before. She suppressed a shiver, thinking of the big ugly rodent that had found a home in her house. When would the exterminator arrive? She'd ask Andy again, but he was a little distracted right now, dealing with another problem. He was dressed in blue jeans and a faded green T-shirt, holding a mug of coffee as he talked with Bert, their ranch hand, who was standing just inside the kitchen at the back door.

"That makes no sense, Bert. Cattle don't just disappear. Someone had to have come in here. You're telling me I'm now missing another five longhorns?"

"From what I can tell, yes. I don't know how, because no one has come in here, and I've been here the entire time. You have that gate out at the north end, but it was latched and secured when I checked. Maybe we should lock it."

She was watching Andy and how worked up he was getting. He was not a man someone could steal from. Whoever was sneaking in here was going to be in some serious trouble. She had no doubt he would hunt down whoever this was and take care of him.

Andy glanced toward her and set down his coffee mug on the counter. His expression told her he didn't believe Bert.

"Maybe it's time you called the sheriff, Andy, get him out here," Laura said.

At one time, she knew he'd never have considered listening to her or any advice she offered. She had also never stepped into his running of this ranch, mainly because she hadn't a clue about cattle or what it took to raise them or sell them to market. This was all Andy.

He nodded, though, his lips firmed white. Yeah, he really was mad.

"I don't know what you think the sheriff is going to do, but hey, get him out here," Bert said. "Maybe he can figure out how they're getting out, because I sure as hell can't." He was sounding really defensive, but then, she supposed he had every right to, considering Andy's longhorns were disappearing on his watch. "Short of camping out in the north field with a shotgun, there's no way to find out what's going on. Might as well lock that gate."

Andy was shaking his head, and she knew that look. He was trying to figure something out. "Sounds to me like someone is on the other side there, taking them. Have you checked that out, Bert?"

Bert seemed surprised. He even glanced Laura's way, which wouldn't earn him any points with Andy. "Hey, I couldn't see any longhorns on that side or I would have gone in there. It's not your property, either, so I'm pretty sure it would be trespassing. But it's not me taking them, Andy. As if I'd have time to be sneaking off with longhorns —and where would I stash them?"

She wasn't sure what Andy was going to say as he grabbed at the back of his neck, rubbing it a little harder than he normally would. She didn't want Bert up and quitting, as she liked the man. He was helpful with the kids, and she never worried when Andy was gone, knowing he'd look after all the livestock. "Andy, why don't you go into town now and get that lock?" she said.

He didn't say anything for a minute as he turned to her, frowning. Maybe he knew what she was doing. When he turned back to Bert, he said, "I've got a feed order coming in. Can you get the shed ready so it can be stored?"

Bert didn't say anything else, just left and headed toward the barn.

Andy watched him through the door, and Laura walked over to him, sliding her hand over his arm, pressing close to him until he was looking down on her. "You don't think he's responsible?"

His blue eyes softened a bit. He seemed to be thinking what to say and then shook his head. "I don't know what to think. Would hate to learn he was, but it seems too easy. He could be. He was here. I don't want to believe he'd steal from me, or to learn I had some thief here with you and the kids."

"Well, what are you going to do?" She knew he wouldn't sit by and do nothing.

"I'm going to buy a lock, ride out, and put it on the gate, maybe camp out for a bit and see who shows up."

"And if they don't come back?"

He took a deep breath, and she felt some of his tension

return. "Then I guess Bert just tipped off whoever's been taking my longhorns."

She really hoped it wasn't so, even though she wasn't keen on Andy confronting some cattle rustlers. She also knew she'd never be able to stop him.

He took her chin in his hands and held her, forcing her to look up at him. "I'll be fine."

"Call the sheriff," she said again, but he was already shaking his head. "Andy, please. I don't want anything to happen to you, and going out there, confronting some thugs, you could get hurt. It's not worth it. None of that is worth something happening to you." She wanted him to reconsider.

For the first time ever, he didn't dismiss her worries and walk out the door. He really looked at her as if he had finally understood what she was saying. He sighed and shut his eyes for a second. "Okay," he said.

"Really, you'll leave this to the sheriff?"

"I'll call him, but I'm still going out there." He leaned in and kissed her. "And I'll take my shotgun."

This time, he reached for his truck keys and paused at the door. "Call Kim, see if she can come and keep you company today," he said, and then he left, was in his pickup, and honked the horn once before he drove away.

Chapter 28

Maybe he was going soft, but seeing the worry in Laura's face made him realize that although they weren't poor, if something happened to him, he didn't want her to struggle, not ever again. Walking away from the fortune had been the only answer, because choosing between the money and his wife and Gabriel wasn't a choice, so he'd find another way, having learned that money couldn't buy love, happiness, or the family he'd created.

He turned his horse, Ladystar, and stopped at the slope of the hill, looking back at the house where his twins were playing, his baby was sleeping, and Laura was waiting. Gabriel was at school and would be back in a few hours on the bus.

In the distance, dust rose from a vehicle, and as he waited, it became clear it was Kim's truck. Knowing Laura wasn't alone with a cattle thief roaming around made him feel a little better, so he turned Ladystar and kicked her up into a trot to make his way to the north end of the field.

He tied her to the fencepost and reached into his

saddlebag to take out the new padlock, then took a look at the gate, which was latched and secure. There was no way it could've blown open. It had to have been opened by someone and closed again after. Andy opened it and walked through, taking a look at the ground. He was sure he was looking at prints from his cattle. Even though the ground was dry from the warm weather they'd had this fall, with no rain in months, those steers were a thousand plus pounds and then some of beefy weight, and that would leave a mark. It looked as if they'd come this way.

As Andy looked out into the distance, he tried to figure out who the thief could be. The open land here went for miles before the heavy forests and parkland began. He knew the neighboring property had been on the market for as long as he'd been here, the owner an eighty-seven-year-old hermit who'd passed away in his sleep one night only to be discovered by a neighbor several days later. As far as he knew, the property still hadn't sold.

Andy slipped his cell phone from his back pocket and called home.

"Andy?" Laura said, answering on the first ring.

"Hey, listen, you don't remember hearing if the property that backs onto the north field owned by that old guy has sold yet, do you?" Why was it he couldn't remember the man's name?

"You mean Clifton Barkley?" she said. "No, I haven't heard. Let me ask Kim."

He smiled, because Laura surprised him more and more with what she remembered, the details she picked up on. At one time, he'd never have asked her. What a fool he'd been for thinking so little of her.

He could hear talking in the background as he stared out, looking for something, any movement at all, but there was nothing.

"Andy, Kim said it's still for sale and no one is living there," Laura said.

As he looked, though, he could see something that told a different story: smoke, not heavy but from someone's fireplace. It was faint, but he was positive now that was what he was seeing.

"Okay, but I'm going to ride over and check something out," he said. He stopped himself from sharing more, because Laura would worry.

"Andy, how long are you going to be?"

"Just long enough to ride down. I'll call you after I check things out."

"Be careful, Andy. Maybe you should call the sheriff again."

The sheriff, whom he'd stopped in town to see after buying the new lock, had taken his information but hadn't seemed too interested in hurrying out to see anything, only mentioning he would at some point check it out. Whatever that meant, Andy wasn't sure, and he realized what everyone else must have felt to have no pull with the local sheriff.

"He knows already," he said. "It'll be fine. Don't worry."

He hung up before she could question him any more. She was smart, intuitive, and she read him better than anyone ever had. He wasn't sure that was such a good thing, though, as he smiled to himself, thinking of her warmth and softness and how much he loved being with her.

Then he mounted Ladystar after closing the gate behind him and started off into the valley to check out who or what was squatting on the old man's land.

Chapter 29

"I always know he's hiding something when he cuts me off like that," Laura said as she hung up the phone and set it back in the cradle, taking in Kim, who looked as if she hadn't heard one word as she cradled Sarah in her arms.

She did look up then, raising her eyebrows. "Andy is an interesting man. I've never met a man who'd walk through fire for his family, for his wife. I always envied you for that, and for him keeping things from you so you won't worry. Well, all I can say is that you just need to be smarter and find out what's going on."

Maybe Kim didn't understand. "Andy wouldn't like sneaky bullshit, especially from women. Sneaking around behind his back isn't something I could do."

"That's not what I'm saying. Sneaking around isn't the answer, but getting on a horse now and joining your husband while he rides out would be more like finding out what he's not telling you."

Was she crazy? Laura could ride a horse, though not

comfortably the way Andy could, as she was still new to this crazy sport her husband loved. "I have children, a baby, and I've never ridden without Andy. It's been a long time since I was on a horse."

"Well, for one, I'm here and will stay with the kids; two, I know horses, and the ones your husband bought for you and Gabriel are two of the gentlest mounts I've ever seen. But if you're afraid, maybe you should stay here."

Laura pulled her lower lip between her teeth, thinking more and more about riding out there to Andy. She would then be able to find out what was going on. "You're sure you'd be okay with the kids, the baby?"

Kim gave her a look as if she should know better. "Of course. Just leave me some milk for the baby so I can feed her, and take your cell phone. Let Bert get you saddled up, and go surprise your husband."

She really shouldn't, but as she stared at the door and the sunshine, thinking of Andy, she didn't allow herself a moment to hesitate. "Okay, I'll do it. Let me pump some milk to leave with you, and I'll ask Bert to saddle up a horse for me." She reached for the new key to the lock Andy was planning on installing on the gate and lifted it from the hook, tucking it into her pocket in case she needed it. "I'll go find Andy. He's going to be mad." She wondered whether Kim had any idea how he could be at times.

"Once he gets past his worry that something could have happened to you and sees how capable you are, he'll be happy to see you. Trust me on this."

Who was she kidding? Andy would be furious. At times, he treated her as if she would break, and she felt as if he had wrapped her in a cocoon, trying to keep every bad thing from her. It was endearing, though, and she had no doubt he loved her deeply, just as she loved him.

No, her husband was just going to have to learn that she wasn't as breakable as he believed.

Chapter 30

H e touched the shotgun tucked in behind his saddle
as he rode closer to the rundown small house the
old man had died in. Smoke rose from the stovepipe in the
roof. Someone was definitely there. He glanced around as
he rode closer, seeing a shed, some old farm buildings, and
scattered broken-down machinery. He stopped, looking
through a break in the trees after hearing a familiar sound,
and that was when he spied a longhorn. He was sure that
closer inspection would only confirm what he already
knew. It was one of his missing cattle.

Then the door opened, and the only thing he could see
was a shotgun pointed his way. In those few seconds as he
hit the ground, leaving Laura alone to raise his children
and what could happen to her were all he could think of.

"Put the gun down!" Andy shouted.

"I don't know who you are, but you get back on your
horse and get the hell out of here. You're trespassing."

He lifted his head when he realized it was a woman's
voice, but he couldn't see much from where he was lying,

his horse grazing a few feet away with his shotgun still tucked in behind the saddle.

"I own the property next to this and saw the smoke. Came to see who was here, as I didn't know the property had been sold." He didn't want to add that his missing cattle were here and he never in a million years would have considered a woman as a potential cattle thief.

"Great, now you've seen. Get on out of here."

She wasn't very tall from what he could tell, her light hair pulled up in a messy bun, wearing a bulky overcoat.

A child ran out, yelling, "Mama, who's here?" It was a boy, maybe eight or ten. He couldn't tell, as the woman was still holding the shotgun and telling her child to get back in the house.

"Didn't mean to scare you," Andy said. "If you'll just lower that gun, I'm not here to hurt you." He should have been angry, but what he thought had happened to his disappearing stock was turning into a picture he'd never have expected. He had questions—a lot of questions.

She lowered the shotgun, pointing it to the ground, but didn't step off the covered porch. Andy slowly got up and walked over to Ladystar without taking his eyes off the woman. He grabbed the reins, and instead of getting on his horse and riding away, he just watched her for a minute. "Don't shoot me," he said. "I'm walking toward you."

She started to raise her shotgun, and he stopped.

"Seriously, I mean you no harm. My family, friends, and the sheriff know I'm here, so don't shoot me."

The sheriff didn't know he was here, as a matter of fact, because he'd had no intention of telling the man, who didn't seem too interested in making his missing cattle a priority. He could see her hesitate and lower the gun again. Her hand was trembling, he could tell, as he got closer. He stopped just at the foot of the stairs, seeing how white her hand was as it held the gun. He wondered whether she knew how to use it, and he feared she could accidentally shoot him if he wasn't careful.

"The name's Andy Friessen. I own the spread next to you with my wife and kids."

He didn't know how old she was. Even though there were threads of gray in her hair, he didn't think she was that old. She had haunted dark eyes. It wasn't the kind of look that scared him as much as bothered him because he didn't know the story there.

"Brandyne," she said abruptly as if she had no intention of lingering.

He gestured with his head to the door. "You have a family, a husband?" he asked, trying to figure out who she was and what she was doing here.

"Look, I don't want any trouble and am not looking for chitchat, so if you'll be on your way," she said. He could hear footsteps and looked past her shoulder to little faces staring out the window: four of them, and he couldn't be sure, but they appeared frightened.

Then everything happened quickly. A horse neighed.

"Andy!" he heard Laura call out as the woman raised her shotgun, and Andy dove in her direction, taking her down as a shot ripped through the air.

Chapter 31

Her heart was racing as she held on to the saddle horn. She hadn't fallen off, but she'd lost one rein. She still had the other, remembering Andy's lessons about what to do for an emergency stop. She pulled the rein all the way back past her hip, keeping it low, turning the horse's head so it was forced to stop and circle. Her leg was shaking as she leaned down and grabbed the other rein, feeling for a moment that she'd fall off. She looked up, her adrenaline pumping, fearing the worst: a gun, a shot, and her husband in the middle of it.

"Laura!" she heard Andy shout.

"I'm okay," she called back and breathed a sigh of relief, starting back to the house, seeing Andy now holding a shotgun as she rode the skittish horse toward him. He was watching her and someone on the porch. As she got closer to Andy, she could see he wasn't happy. No, he was downright mad, and she couldn't be sure if it was at her or the person who'd fired off that shot.

"What the hell are you doing here?" Oh yeah, he was

mad at her, the way he snapped. Then she noticed the scrape on his cheek.

"Are you okay? Who's that?" she said. Andy reached out and grabbed the reins, holding the horse while she climbed down. She reached up and touched his face. "You're hurt."

He shook his head, holding the horse and then glancing back at the house. "I'm fine, but why the hell are you riding in here when I'm dealing with this crazy person? You could have been shot or worse, killed, and then what the hell would I do? This isn't just you and me. There's the kids, too. What would they do without you?" He was yelling, and at one time this would have scared her, how close to losing it he was, but she could see how upset this had made him, and it was about so much more than him trying to protect his family.

"I'm okay. You can be mad at me later, but what's going on here?" she asked, taking in the old house, having never seen this property up close, thinking now Kim must have been wrong about the property still being up for sale. "Who's living here?"

She could see he was trying to dial it back and figure out what to do next. He had always been able to think on the spot. This was the first time she'd ever seen him truly rattled.

"I don't know who she is, but there're kids here, too."

Laura looked up to a woman standing on the porch, little faces hiding behind her. "Hello, I'm Andy's wife, Laura," she said. She lifted her hand as she stepped around Andy.

"What the hell, Laura?" He grabbed her arm and was trying to stick her behind him.

"I'm sorry," the woman said. "The gun went off by accident. I didn't mean for it to."

"You could have shot my wife," Andy snapped again, taking a step closer, and Laura walked beside him and then touched his arm, because her husband was being anything but friendly with this woman.

"I'm sorry, it was an accident," she said again, then shushed her children, who sounded frightened. Laura couldn't tell how many there were, three or four.

"I'm okay," she said. "No harm done." Andy made a sound of pure disgust, and she glanced up at him and repeated herself: "I'm okay. Let's just find out who she is, and the kids." She gestured as they got closer. She could see the children, their worn dirty clothes, looking skinny and unsure at the same time. She understood that look, and it tugged at her heart. "Are you alone here?"

"Look, I don't want trouble, and I told your husband to just turn around and leave us be."

"Mama!" An older girl was in the doorway, maybe in her early teens, with short dark hair, wearing an old tattered sweater over blue jeans.

"Go back inside," the woman said to the girl as the sound of a vehicle pulling in had them all glancing out. It was the sheriff.

That was when Laura's stomach dropped, and she saw the uncertainty of this family turn to fear. The young girl's face paled. Laura understood it all too well.

Andy turned to her then. "Are you squatting here?" he asked.

The woman looked right at him and said, "Not exactly."

Chapter 32

The fact was that his cattle were here on this property with a woman and five children who looked as if they had barely anything to scrape together, let alone eat. He looked at the blankets on the floor in the living room as if the kids had all crowded in to sleep. The house had an old sofa, a small wooden kitchen table with two chairs, and an empty bedroom. There appeared to be scraps of things left on the table, and something was simmering in a pot on the woodstove. He hoped she hadn't butchered one of the cattle, but then, he couldn't believe a woman would have the strength to pull something like that off.

"So Clifton was your father-in-law?" the sheriff asked the woman, who had said her name was Brandyne, as Laura took in the squalor and stepped closer to Andy. He didn't miss the shiver she suppressed, and he wondered whether she was thinking of the hard times she'd lived through.

"No, he wasn't. My husband—I mean, Willy and me weren't married, but he's my kids' daddy, and this was his father's place." Brandyne had an arm around two of her young children. The youngest appeared about three or four, from what he could tell.

"Then how about you explain to me how this is, because as it's looking now, you've stolen cattle belonging to Mr. Friessen here, and you're squatting, and both of these mean I'm going to need to take you in."

One of the kids started crying.

"Andy, you can't let this happen," Laura pleaded. "Do something."

"What am I supposed to do? This isn't looking too good for her."

Laura was shaking her head, and whatever she was thinking, he knew she was right about a few things. They didn't have all the answers, but the sheriff hauling this woman off could be really bad, and then what would happen to her children?

"Where is this Willy?" Andy asked, wondering why he wasn't here looking after his family.

"I don't know. He left us in the next town at the park, said he'd be back after he made some calls. He never came back."

"How long ago was this?" Laura was beside him again, holding his arm.

"About a month ago." Her children were staring at the sheriff and then Andy as if they didn't know who to be more scared of. "I asked around then, and no one had seen him. I didn't have much money and couldn't afford a motel room, so I thought maybe Willy came out here to his dad's place, but when I found out in town that Clifton had died and the property was just sitting here empty, I thought at least we had a place to stay until Willy showed up."

"Sheriff, did Clifton have a son?" Andy asked, and the sheriff was shaking his head.

"Could have. I don't know for sure. Clifton kept to

himself, but she's still trespassing, and then there's your cattle."

Laura squeezed his arm.

"I didn't know they were yours," the older girl said. "They were by the gate, and they looked like they wanted to be on this side, grazing."

Her mother turned to her, eyes flashing. "You didn't tell me that part, Rita! You opened a gate? You told me they were just grazing. I wouldn't steal cattle. I thought maybe they belonged to Willy's dad."

"I didn't know! I'm sorry. It was just a gate I opened. Please don't take my mom away," the teen pleaded, and one of the kids started crying.

"Sheriff, I'm not pressing charges here," Andy said. Considering the circumstances, he couldn't see a family torn apart by some bad choices. "The gate really isn't very secure, so I can see how this could have happened." The fact was that the gate had been closed after she let the cattle out, and he was pretty sure he wasn't being told the entire story, but now wasn't the time to ask.

"Okay," the sheriff said, glancing his way, taking off his hat and running his fingers through his thick dark hair. "But that still leaves you squatting here. This property's for sale, and unless you have something that says Clifton was passing this on to Willy…a will, a deed, something?"

She swallowed, and he could see the sheen of tears and desperation in her expression. "I don't. All I know is that Willy said this was his dad's place. We don't have any place to go."

"Andy," Laura pleaded, and he understood well how her heart went out to this woman.

"The sheriff's right, Laura. Brandyne, you can't stay here. There's no electricity, this place needs so much work, and you have what for food?" Andy said, looking around at the emptiness and sparseness of the abandoned home. They had managed to find enough wood to burn in the woodstove, he could see, so they had heat and could cook, but this wasn't an ideal situation. Willy was half the man he should have been. He should have been there, looking after his family. Instead, Andy was pretty sure the loser had cut his losses and left town to start over somewhere else.

"Okay, we'll go," Brandyne said.

"No," the sheriff said. "Where are you planning on going?"

"Maybe they could stay with us," Laura said, and Andy groaned, thinking of where they'd stick them—but he knew his wife wasn't about to turn her back on someone in need. No more than he could, if truth be told.

"Well, that's mighty neighborly, ma'am." The sheriff glanced back at Andy, and he had to look down at Laura and the empathy she had for this family.

"Absolutely, until something can be figured out," he said. "At least for tonight, they can stay with us." He realized even as Laura threw her arms around his neck, hugging him and kissing him, that helping out this mother and her children was the right thing to do.

"Well, that's mighty fine," the sheriff added as he stepped up to Andy and put his hand on his shoulder, and it was then that Andy saw that this sheriff, who had seemed too busy to look for Andy's cattle, suddenly appreciated this gesture. "Mr. Friessen, it's been a pleasure," he said.

Chapter 33

B randyne and her five children had stayed for four nights crowded into two rooms, the guestroom and Gabriel's. Gabriel had been moved into the twins' bedroom on an air mattress on the floor, and it was in those five days and four nights that the exterminator had shown up and trapped the rat, the drywaller had put in the new ceiling, and Andy and Laura had learned that Brandyne, now thirty-two, had fallen for a rodeo star in high school and had her first child, Rita, at eighteen in Wyoming. The next four, Colton, Hadley, Nora, and Emma, the baby, who was only three, had all been born on the road traveling from rodeo to rodeo. Willy was now a washed-up bronc rider.

The kids had been skin and bones, and Brandyne not much better. The first meal Laura and Andy had cooked for them was chicken, baked potatoes, corn, and a salad Kim had thrown together, having also stayed when she'd learned of the young family's plight. Brandyne and her children had looked at the food longingly in a way Laura had once done. She had lived that hunger, she had lived with nothing, and she realized as she watched them, unsure and polite through those first bites, that she was no longer carrying the fear that she could end up that way again.

"Hey, what are you thinking?" Andy slid his hand over her stomach, pulling her back against him as she stared out at the sunset and the last of the neighbors who had just left after putting together a community potluck to help the young mother and her children.

A house in town had been offered to the family rent free until Brandyne could get back on her feet, and many of the folks in Kim's church had provided everything else the young mother needed: food, clothing, blankets, dishes, and a few dollars to tide her over. Laura had to fight tears at their kindness, but it was the sheriff who had surprised them all, a single man who had befriended Brandyne.

"Who knew there are actually communities that help their neighbors? I never would have believed people could open their hearts like the people in this community have. The generosity, the love. If only…" She stopped talking as she thought back to when she had lost everything, living in her car with her little boy, struggling to stay warm.

"What?" He slid his other arm around her chest, and she held on to him as he leaned down and kissed her neck. "If only what?"

She turned around, slipping her arms around his neck, pressing into all his warmth and love. "I was going to say if only I'd had the same help, but I just realized I would never have had you then. Despite how bad it was, and it was awful, I would go through it all again to have you." She slid her hands over his cheeks and took in the awe in his expression. "I love you so much, Andy Friessen. My heart is so full. Thank you for moving us to be here with these people, these friends, and thank you for loving me."

And she kissed him, opening up to this man, her husband, who was her everything.

Turn the page for a sneak peek of
THE PROMISE the next book in THE FRIESSENS
Available in print, audio, eBook.

Falling in love with Jed Friessen was a dream come true.

Married to Jed, Diana has a family and is living her happily ever after. She knew heartbreak and suffering as a child, and the pain of rejection, but she now understands what it means to be loved.

However, when the past comes knocking on her door, reminding her of everything she's left behind, everything she was, and everything she's lost, her guilt and doubt threaten the life she's built with her husband.

Chapter 1

There were two realities. The first was her picture-perfect life in the countryside on a ranch with her handsome and overly protective husband, Jed, and their two little boys, Danny, five, and Christopher, three. It was her happily ever after, and nothing bad could ever touch her there. In the second, Diana Friessen, daughter of the town whore, would forever be tainted by the sins of her mother, always having to remind herself she was worthy of being loved.

It was difficult, if not downright impossible some days, to process her past, which she had long since separated from the person she was now. Who was Diana Friessen? She had defined herself for so long by surviving, by carrying the weight of someone else's wrongs. She had brought that weight into her picture, making the ache, the pain, and the hurt part of her story until she left, only to return years later and be swept off her feet by love.

She was loved by Jed. She could see how much she was a part of him from the moments they spent together and everything he did for her. He wanted—no, needed to have her here at home, raising his boys. She had once believed this was because he didn't want to compete with her career, and truth be told, Jed was not a man who could ever come second. He wasn't made that way, and she didn't think she could love a man who could settle for the bits and pieces tossed his way. He was her everything, and she'd given up all she'd chosen just to be his. He had built a business conducting horse clinics, working with children, some with special needs. He was an amazing man, and he filled her with such hope and completeness that she would never have loneliness as her bed partner again.

She'd give it all up again, too, even though she loved knowing she had a law degree, an achievement all her own, and she could begin a practice at any time. It was something she'd begun thinking of more and more as of late: having something that was just hers.

"What are you thinking?" Jed slid his hand around her stomach, pulling her against him so she could feel all his hardness and the way his amazing body molded against hers. They were made for each other, and she loved how she fit him so perfectly, comfortably. He pressed his cheek, which was rough with whiskers from two days without shaving, against hers.

She reached her hand back to touch him, his face, his head, as he held her as he always did, in a way that let her know he'd never let her fall.

"Oh, life and things," she said as he kissed her cheek, and of course she smiled, as being loved by Jed was something she had to remind herself every day never to take for granted. He gave her all of himself.

"Tell me," he said without letting her go as she swayed against him.

"I was thinking of a lot of things, how you make me feel safe, and for so long I've felt as if I could finally heal, knowing you were taking care of everything, me and the kids, and just being loved by you." She sighed, and he didn't say anything but slid his other arm around her front, over her breasts, and then held her shoulder, wrapping her up in him so she could touch his wrist and hold on. "I realized, too, I'm not who I used to be."

"Sounds like you're bothered by something." He kissed her cheek again as she breathed deeply, relaxing.

"Not so much bothered but considering." She noticed a car coming down their long driveway in the distance. With the dust and the fact that they lived so far out of town on flat land she could see for miles, no one could sneak up on them. "You expecting anyone?" She started to straighten when Jed stepped to her side, sliding his hand around her hip, holding her to him.

"No," he replied.

She didn't say anything else, her stomach knotting at the sight of a faded blue compact.

For a minute, she wished Jed would say something, because he had to know how uncomfortable she was. The man could read her like no other, and she couldn't hide anything from him.

"Isn't that…?" He stopped, frowning, as the car pulled up in front of the small house, zipping in beside Diana's SUV.

Diana's hand slid up to her throat on instinct. She wasn't sure whether she had gasped until Jed touched her arm, drawing her gaze to him. She hadn't realized he'd been watching her.

"I can't believe this. Your mother is back. What the hell is she thinking, after I sent her on her way?" Jed sounded really mad, and Diana didn't have a chance to answer when the car door shut.

"Oh, hi there!" Faye Claremont said as she darted

around the front of the car in a light blue T-shirt and matching pencil skirt, wearing inch-high sandals. Her deep red hair was brushed back into a ponytail, her lips painted bright red, and she had a curvy body that screamed sex. "Well, just looky here at all you've done to this place. It's looking mighty fine from when I was here last." She stopped at the bottom of the stairs, taking in the one-story house and the addition Jed had built. It had white siding, green trim, and a front deck with a finished railing. Diana wanted to scream at her to shut up.

Jed said nothing as he glanced between Diana and her mother. "And when exactly was that?" he asked. For a moment, Faye's bright vivid smile faltered before she stepped on the bottom of the stairs.

"Why, just last week. Didn't Diana tell you I stopped by?"

She could feel Jed's fingers digging in to her hips, holding her to him as she touched the railing of the front deck, which looked over the acres of flat land. She looked away to the barn and indoor arena where Jed held his clinics. She could hear a horse nicker from the barn, and she swallowed, her tongue thick, unsure of what the hell to say, wishing she could crawl away and hide. Yes, her mother had stopped by not once but twice after how many years? It had rocked Diana's world, and each time had been unannounced. Faye was trying to worm her way back into her life, or so it seemed.

"So what can I do for you, Faye?" Jed said, not giving a hint that somehow, he and Diana could keep secrets from each other.

"Well, I wanted to see my daughter and try to make amends, and I feel as if we're making some real progress. Ain't that right, baby?" Faye smiled brightly to Diana, and she wondered whether Jed could hear the strangled noise she was making or if it was all in her head.

"Faye, I made it very clear to you the first time that you're not to come back here. I don't want you coming around here, upsetting my wife." Jed was quite direct, and Diana also knew he'd likely have a word or two with her later. The overwhelming guilt ate away at her, because she hadn't shared with Jed the fact that Faye Claremont had ignored his decree and kept coming back. Even now, she couldn't explain why.

"That isn't my intention. It was never my intent to cause any upset to my daughter, and I feel honestly that we were making progress." She was looking toward Diana, and this time Jed was also staring down at her.

"Why do you keep coming here? I didn't ask you to come." Diana had finally found her voice, and it sounded so strange, so weak.

"I need to make amends, and I told you that. I can't even begin to make things right after what happened, being taken from you. I just had a lot of years to think about it, and you're my daughter. No matter what's happened, I know there's no excuse for what I put you through. I made a lot of bad choices. I know that now."

"Faye." Jed leaned on the railing, resting on his forearms, looking down on her. He was no longer touching Diana, but he hadn't moved from her side. "I appreciate you wanting to make amends to my wife, but I was also clear that you weren't to come back here and were to leave my wife be. I don't take kindly to anyone messing with my wife, hurting her, upsetting her. You understand that your bridge here has already burned." He said it so calmly and flicked his hand toward her, but there was no mistaking his meaning.

Faye flashed her big blue eyes, smiling up at him. What

was she thinking, trying to turn the charm on Diana's husband? Maybe she realized her mistake, as she suddenly dialed it back a bit. This was the first time she'd had a chance to admire Jed, to ogle him, but she must have understood clearly that Jed was not the man for her to be setting her sights on. Diana wanted to smack her for crossing that line.

"You're a very lucky woman, Diana, to have a husband like the one you have. I'd have given anything for it, but it wasn't in the cards for me. I did the best I could, and maybe that wasn't good enough. It was what it was." She opened her purse and pulled out a pamphlet, then stepped closer and held it out, but Jed reached around Diana and took it. She couldn't make herself look at it, just stared at the woman who'd given birth to her, whom Diana favored, who'd made her childhood hell and made her doubt everything good in her life.

"It's my group." Faye gestured to the paper Jed was holding. "We meet on Thursdays, and I'd really like you to come." Instead of pushing, going on and on as she always had about everything, her life and her crap, she stepped back, looking sadly over at Diana before turning and walking back to her car, where she slid behind the wheel.

As Faye drove away, leaving a trail of dust behind her, Jed turned to Diana and said, "So how about you explain why you lied to me?"

About the Author

With flawed strong characters, characters you can relate to, New York Times & USA Today Bestselling Author Lorhainne Eckhart writes the kind of books she wants to read. She is frequently a Top 100 bestselling author in multiple genres, and her second book ever published, The Forgotten Child, is no exception. With close to 900 reviews on Amazon, translated into German and French, this book was such a hit that the long running Friessen Family series was born. Now with over sixty titles and multiple series under her belt her big family romance series are loved by fans worldwide. A recipient of the 2013, 2015 and 2016 Readers' Favorite Award for Suspense and Romance, Lorhainne lives on the sunny west-coast Gulf Island of Salt Spring Island, is the mother of three, her oldest has autism and she is an advocate for never giving up on your dreams.

Lorhainne loves to hear from her readers! You can connect with me at:
www.LorhainneEckhart.com
Lorhainne@LorhainneEckhart.com

Also by Lorhainne Eckhart

The Outsider Series

The Forgotten Child (Brad and Emily)

A Baby and a Wedding (An Outsider Series Short)

Fallen Hero (Andy, Jed, and Diana)

The Search (An Outsider Series Short)

The Awakening (Andy and Laura)

Secrets (Jed and Diana)

Runaway (Andy and Laura)

Overdue (An Outsider Series Short)

The Unexpected Storm (Neil and Candy)

The Wedding (Neil and Candy)

The Friessens: A New Beginning

The Deadline (Andy and Laura)

The Price to Love (Neil and Candy)

A Different Kind of Love (Brad and Emily)

A Vow of Love, A Friessen Family Christmas

The Friessens

The Reunion

The Bloodline (Andy & Laura)

The Promise (Diana & Jed)

The Business Plan (Neil & Candy)

The Decision (Brad & Emily)

First Love (Katy)

Family First

Leave the Light On

In the Moment

In the Family

In the Silence

In the Stars

In the Charm

Unexpected Consequences

It Was Always You

The First Time I Saw You

Welcome to My Arms

I'll Always Love You

The McCabe Brothers

Don't Stop Me (Vic)

Don't Catch Me (Chase)

Don't Run From Me (Aaron)

Don't Hide From Me (Luc)

Don't Leave Me (Claudia)

The Wilde Brothers

The One (Joe and Margaret)

The Honeymoon, A Wilde Brothers Short

Friendly Fire (Logan and Julia)

Not Quite Married, A Wilde Brothers Short

A Matter of Trust (Ben and Carrie)

Made in the USA
Middletown, DE
28 August 2019